Other Books by Lois Lenski

Autobiographical

A LITTLE GIRL OF NINETEEN HUNDRED

Historical

PHEBE FAIRCHILD, HER BOOK
A-GOING TO THE WESTWARD
BOUND GIRL OF COBBLE HILL
OCEAN-BORN MARY
INDIAN CAPTIVE
BLUEBERRY CORNERS
PURITAN ADVENTURE

Regional

BAYOU SUZETTE
STRAWBERRY GIRL
BLUE RIDGE BILLY
JUDY'S JOURNEY
BOOM TOWN BOY
COTTON IN MY SACK
TEXAS TOMBOY
PRAIRIE SCHOOL
MAMA HATTIE'S GIRL
CORN FARM BOY
SAN FRANCISCO BOY
FLOOD FRIDAY
HOUSEBOAT GIRL
COAL CAMP GIRL

CORN-FARM BOY

CORN~FARM BOY

by
LOIS LENSKI

J.B. Lippincott Company
Philadelphia ~ New York

For
my corn-farm children,
with love

FOREWORD

The fact that American children are carrying on this series of Regional books has been very gratifying to me. I am continually receiving suggestions from child readers for new locations. They write, "Come and see where we live and what we do. Please come and write about us."

My choice of Iowa for a corn story came about in this way. In the fall of 1951, city children in Cedar Rapids, Iowa, wrote me suggesting a corn story. One little girl said, "My grandfather lives on a farm and has lots of troubles"—which she wanted to tell me about. I replied that if I wrote such a story, I would need the help of real corn-farm children.

Such help came soon afterwards, when the children of a rural school, Henry No. 5, in Plymouth County, began writing me under the guidance of their teacher, Mrs. Celeste Frank. They took me, through letters and drawings sent over two winters, into the very heart of their lives, describing outward details of farm life and especially the way they themselves lived, worked and played.

Through the help of an Iowa women's radio program, news began to circulate through the state that I was looking for material for a "corn story." The radio brought me letters from corn-farm housewives, among them: Mrs. Lloyd Dougal, Mrs. Opal Winship, Mrs. Carrie Wiggans and many others. These women were helpful in interpreting the woman's point of view.

Children in other schools began to write—Graettinger, Kalma, Otho, Oskaloosa, Manning, Rose Hill, Doon, Blockton and Rising City, Nebraska. Some schools sent historical material, others statistics about corn and farm products, or publicity booklets and guidebooks. What I wanted most and found hardest to get were stories of the everyday life of the corn-farm child. It was difficult for teachers to understand that the child's everyday life in his own family, as lived today *instead of in the past, was important enough to become the contents of a book.*

The Plymouth County children made an outstanding contribution. To them and their teacher go my sincere thanks and appreciation. When I spent the month of July 1953 in Iowa, I visited them in their homes, came

FOREWORD

to know and love them and their families, and learned many things I could not have learned by correspondence or research. I could now visualize my characters, as my composite family grew in my imagination, and place them in an authentic setting. The children themselves benefited by the whole experience—their gift for expressing themselves in the language and graphic arts increased through their interest in the project. Most of all, they acquired a new evaluation of the significance of their own daily lives as a vital strand in the warp and woof of the American pattern of living.

In Iowa I saw the peak of the corn-growing season. I thrilled over the sheer beauty of the countryside with its rolling hills and patchwork squares of rich green and gold-colored fields. I rode tractors, walked between the dark rows of tall hybrid corn then bursting into tassel, and watched the combining of oats in the hot bright sunshine. I felt a pronounced regional feeling in this northwest corner of the state, indigenous in its agricultural economy. I sensed how deeply the children's lives grew out of their environment.

Two eleven-year-old boys were invaluable in the help they gave me— Noel Leinen and Ronald Dougal. From them I learned how a corn-farm boy thinks and feels as well as what he does outwardly. They acquainted me not only with the joys and humor of farm life, but also with its sorrows, hazards and danger, for with these they lived closely, too. Their frankness, honesty and confidence were gratifying.

This book is as true and honest as I could make it. All the incidents have happened in real life to some living person. None are distorted or exaggerated for effect. Pages of conversation were taken down verbatim. No attempt has been made to invent or impose upon my background a synthetic, author-manufactured plot. It is my firm belief that the happenings of daily life, episodic as they may appear, form the only sound basis for plotting an honest story—a story of vital family relationships and the give-and-take of daily life in a chosen setting.

Human life in its basic essence needs no glamorization or exaggeration. It has all the elements of vital drama inherent in itself.

My earnest thanks go to all the men, women and children of this region who contributed of their own experiences to enrich this book.

Lois Lenski

Lutean Shores
Tarpon Springs, Florida
December 18, 1953

CONTENTS

LISTEN TO THE TALL CORN GROW

Song of the Corn-farm Children

Words by Lois Lenski

Music by Clyde Robert Bulla

1. LIS-TEN TO THE TALL CORN GROW, HEAR IT WHIS-PER DOWN THE ROW—
2. OH, JUST WATCH THE TALL CORN SPROUT, SEE THE LEAVES COME POP-PING OUT;
3. ALL DAY LONG IN BLAZ-ING HEAT, ALL NIGHT LONG BE-NEATH A SHEET—

SOFT-LY WHIS-PER ALL NIGHT LONG, SOFT-LY SING ITS GROW-ING SONG.
UP KNEE-HIGH BY FOURTH OF JU-LY, THEN IT'S TIME TO LAY IT BY.
WHAT DOES IT WHIS-PER AN-Y-WAY? WHAT DOES THE TALL CORN TRY TO SAY?

Chorus

ON-LY THE CORN-FARM BOY CAN KNOW WHAT THE TALL CORN SAYS WHEN IT STARTS TO GROW.

ON-LY THE FARM BOY KNOWS IT WELL, AND WHAT HE KNOWS HE'LL NEV-ER TELL.

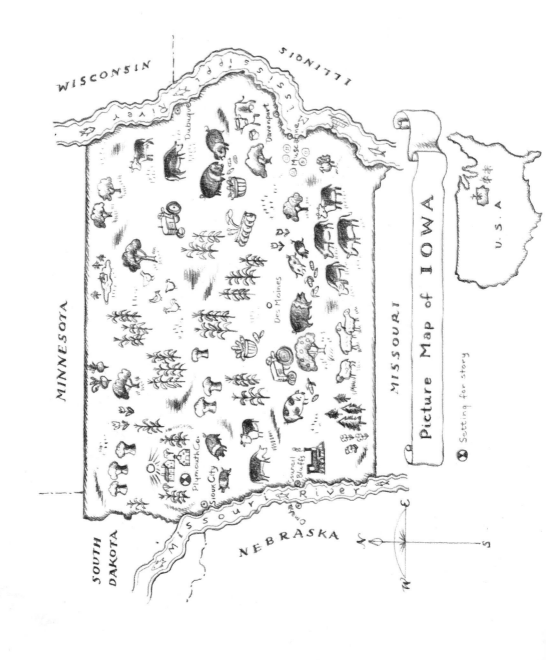

Picture Map of IOWA

(X) Setting for story

CHAPTER I

The New Tractor

"Why, Dick! Why have you come home?"

The boy came into the kitchen and sat down. His mother took a pan of hot rolls from the oven. She looked up, her face flushed from the heat.

"I don't feel so good, Mom," said Dick.

"Did the teacher say you could leave school in the middle of the morning?" asked his mother.

"It was recess," said Dick. "Yes—she said I could go home."

"And you walked?" asked Mom. "All the way?"

"Well—no," said Dick. "Ted Sanders was going by in his pick-up. He gave me a ride."

"But why? What's the matter, Dick?"

"I don't feel so good, Mom. My stomach hurts."

Dick reached over to sample a hot roll.

"No—no fresh bread," said Mom. "Not if your stomach is upset. Go upstairs and get to bed."

"Aw, Mom—not in the middle of the morning," begged Dick. "Is it eleven o'clock yet? Has your clock stopped?"

"Go on upstairs, Dick, and get undressed," said Mom sternly. "I'll come up soon and take your temperature."

Dick threw off his cap and jacket. He climbed the stairs slowly. He would get in bed with his clothes on. He would listen to hear them when they came. Then he would dash down and out the door before Mom could catch him.

The upstairs was only a half-story. It had three bedrooms with sloping ceilings. The one on the west was the boys' room, which Dick shared with his older brother, Raymond. On the wall colored pictures of birds were tacked up. Four small bird books and a natural history stood in an open bookcase, with several birds' nests. On the lower shelves were farm and sports magazines. The bed was still unmade, just as the boys had jumped out of it.

Dick untied his shoestrings. He kicked his shoes off with a great clatter. He ducked under the quilts and pulled them up. He reached for a magazine to read, but it was too dark, for there was only one low window. He pulled the long string he had rigged up. It went from the iron headboard to the light dangling from the ceiling. The light clicked on. He smiled to think how smart he was.

He lay back on the pillows. Gosh! He was really tired. He had walked most of the way, nearly two miles. Ted Sanders had only

[2]

brought him from the corner. Dick just had to get home in time. When were they ever coming? He raised himself on his elbow and looked out the window, but saw no one. Raymond had said they would be back by ten-thirty. Raymond was lucky. He always got to do everything with Dad. He acted as if he were a man already, and he was only sixteen. Dick tried to read, but could not keep his mind on the words. He kept hearing outside noises.

He heard a bird singing—a robin. It was March and the robins were back. How good to think winter was over and spring had come. This year Dick was really going to farm. He could do everything that Raymond could do—as good or even better. If only Dad would let him . . . He knew just as much about a tractor as Raymond did. Dad did not know that whenever he spent a day in town, Raymond let Dick drive. Now, with this new tractor —with two tractors on the place, Dad would need somebody to drive it. He'd show Dad and Uncle Henry how well he could drive.

Steps up the stairway made Dick pull the covers up around his neck. The next minute Mom was in the room, and the thermometer was in his mouth. He could not talk. He could not tell from Mom's face whether she guessed or not.

"I hate to have you down sick today," Mom said. "Just when I want to start spring housecleaning. I have new wallpaper for this room, and the woodwork needs a coat of paint."

She took the thermometer out of the boy's mouth and looked at it.

"No worse than usual," she said. "About half a degree. But I suppose it won't hurt you to stay in bed and rest. I'll make up the girls' bed while I'm upstairs. You'd better take one of your tablets—and I'll fix you some broth for dinner."

[3]

"Mom, where's Margy?" asked Dick.

"I sent her out to the henhouse to get me some eggs," said Mom. She went downstairs and Dick could hear her rattling pans and moving dishes. Dinner would soon be ready. Would they never come?

At last the welcome sound of engine motors came roaring through the open window. In a flash Dick was out of the bed and had his shoes on. Before his mother could call him, he was down the stairs and out the back door. He got there in time, after all.

They were coming up the lane—Dad and Uncle Henry in the pick-up and Raymond behind—on the new tractor. Oh, the lucky bum! He always got to do everything first. Dick flew across the house yard, the gate with its heavy iron weights clanging shut behind him. He was right there by the time they stopped. And in a few minutes, here came Mom and Margy too.

Oh, what a beauty she was! There was nothing more beautiful in the whole world than a brand-new tractor. So graceful, so neat, so streamlined, so powerful—as strong as twenty or thirty horses, think of it! New, shiny green paint without a nick or a mud-speck on it and huge wheels with the big lugs that could take the wonderful machine over hills and streams and mountains—anywhere!

Dick could not find words to express his admiration. He just listened while the others talked. Dad and Raymond and Uncle Henry sang the machine's praises in loud voices.

No one asked Dick why he was not at school. Mom did not scold him for getting out of bed. She did not even act surprised that he had his clothes on. They were all too excited.

"Mighty good of you to buy it, Henry," said Dad. "It sure will help us out with the planting."

[4]

"I just want to speed you slowpokes up a little," laughed Uncle Henry.

Dick's father, Mark Hoffman, was a heavy-set man, twice as strong as Henry Shumaker. Uncle Henry's wife, Aunt Etta, was Dick's mother's sister. Uncle Henry Shumaker was thin and wiry. The Hoffman place was his old home-place, where he grew up as a boy. He lived in town now, because Aunt Etta and the girls liked it better there. He had inherited the farm from Grandfather Shumaker. Now he rented it to Mark Hoffman.

"Show us how she goes, Raymond," said Uncle Henry.

"Gimme a ride! Gimme a ride!" begged Margy.

Margy was only five, but she loved a tractor as much as any one on the farm. She climbed up beside her big brother.

"Don't let her stand," Mom called out. "We don't want an accident the first thing. Take her on your lap, Raymond."

Raymond took the little girl on his lap and drove slowly around the barnyard. Then he got off and Dad tried it.

"Smooth as a whistle!" said Dad, grinning.

"Back to the kitchen for me," cried Mom. "Your dinner's burning up." She ran in, with Margy at her heels.

"Can I try it now, Dad?" asked Dick. "It's my turn, isn't it?"

Mark Hoffman looked down at Dick. His eyes twinkled.

"What makes you think you can drive it, son?"

"Oh well, I . . ." Dick looked at Raymond. "Oh well, I can drive the old one pretty good. Raymond lets me—sometimes."

"Corn-farm kids know how to drive by instinct these days," said Uncle Henry. "They don't need teaching. Let Dick try her."

"Dick's not very strong," began Dad. "He has to be careful."

"Oh, I'm feeling fine now, Dad," bragged Dick.

[5]

"Yoo hoo! Yoo hoo!" Margy stood by the house-yard gate and called, "Dinner! Everybody come to dinner."

Dick turned to the house with the others, disappointed. He hated to leave the beautiful new machine. He wanted to stroke it, as if it were a horse. He had a feeling it might disappear if they all went away and left it.

"Can I? After dinner, Dad?" he begged.

"We'll take her out in the field after dinner," said Uncle Henry, "and give her a real workout." He turned to Mark. "Did the surveyor get your contour all laid out?"

"Yes," said Dad, frowning. "He spent hours and hours at it. He marked all the curves and got us started. It looks crazy to me."

"Got to keep up with the latest tricks," laughed Uncle Henry, "if you want to make a corn farm pay. Contour planting is best on rolling land like this. Instead of rows up and down hill, you plant around the hill, and build grass terraces now and then, to keep the land from washing when it rains."

The men stopped at the cistern pump by the walk. They washed in the basin on the bench back of the house and dried on the towel hanging there. Then they all trooped in. The kitchen was full of the good smells of freshly baked bread, fried steak and boiled cabbage. They sat down at the oilcloth-covered table and ate. Dick ate as much as any one. He had forgotten about feeling sick. And Mom must have forgotten too, for she had not fixed any broth. As soon as Dick finished, he ran upstairs and took off his school clothes. He put on his old shirt and dungarees, then his jacket and cap.

Dick and Raymond went out in the field with the men after dinner. They put the drag on the new tractor and started drag-

[6]

ging. They were still there when Wilma got home from school. Wilma was fourteen and in first year High. She came home from town by bus. After changing into her jeans, she came running out. She got there just in time to see Dick driving. How proud he felt! He waved his hand to her. Dad had unhooked the drag.

Dick liked driving at first, then he was not so sure. He didn't much like the curves. And worse than that, his legs began to ache. He would not tell any one, of course. If he told Mom, she would be sure to put him to bed and keep him there. Dick had laughed at Dad when he said the curves made him dizzy. But now, he felt the same way himself. The engine began to cough a little, so he gave it a little more gas. He turned the wheel to avoid tipping. Did he turn it too far?

The next thing he knew he was going over. He heard the men yelling at him. A big bump and the engine stopped. He kicked,

opened his eyes, and found himself lying sprawled out in the dirt. Dad and Uncle Henry were picking him up. Raymond was taking care of the tractor.

Wilma looked scared. "Did you hurt yourself?" she cried.

Dick got on his feet and felt of his legs and arms. There was no pain, no bruise, nothing.

"I'm O. K.!" he said. "Good thing the ground is soft."

"If you'd a hit a rock with that head of yours," joked Uncle Henry, "you might have broke the rock in two!"

Dad looked serious. "Are you all right, son?"

"Yes, Dad," said Dick. "It didn't hurt me any."

"I guess kids your age had better wait a while to drive," said Dad.

"Aw—Dad . . ." but Dick knew there was no use coaxing now.

The arrival of Uncle Henry's new tractor made it an exciting day. But more excitement came in the evening, after Uncle Henry had driven back to town. Dick did not need to be told that they were in for a night of it. He hoped Dad would not tell Mom how he fell from the tractor. For if he did, Mom would never let him stay up all night. And he was determined to stay up this time. Nobody—nothing was going to stop him. His mind was made up.

It was pig time now. Today was the date to commence. Dad had the date circled with red crayon on his big farm calendar in the kitchen. For two or three weeks in March, they would have a busy time, for the sows would be having their pigs.

Susie, Dick's pet sow, was one of them. She was a Hampshire hog of enormous size, black with a white belt around her waist and a white neckband. Her big ears hung down over her eyes.

They had bought her a month before and Dick had tamed her so he could walk in her pen at any time. When he held out an ear of corn, she came to eat. While she ate, he rubbed her ears and scratched her back. Now she knew him.

Other sows were ready to farrow too. Dick knew because he saw Raymond cleaning and liming the hog-house. He saw Dad hauling bales of straw and ground corncobs for bedding, and feed and water out. Dad had all the partitions and guard rails up and was fixing the straw in the pens already. Raymond had wired the hog-house for electricity during the winter. Now he tested the heat-lamps to see that they were working. Dick knew Dad and Raymond were planning to be up all night.

Wilma helped with the evening chores. Nobody called Dick to help, so he lay down on the sun-porch couch to rest. If he could tell Mom that he had had a rest, she would be more apt to let him stay up. Maybe not all night, but a while anyway. After Susie's pigs came and after Dick made sure she was all right and he knew how many little pigs she had, he would go to bed and let Dad take care of the others.

After the chores were done, Raymond got in the car and went over to see Russell Ruden, a neighbor boy. The argument did not start until bedtime. After Mom put Margy to bed, she called, "Time for bed, Dick."

Dick looked at his father who was reading the paper by the table light. He wondered if Dad would help him out. Wilma was doing her homework. Would she say a good word for him?

Dick called up the stairway, "Aw—can't I stay up a while, Mom? I want to go to the hog-house with Dad. Just for a little while, Mom."

Mom came down the stairs.

"You came home from school half-sick this morning," she said. "You've had a big day, with the new tractor and all. In this damp spring weather, it's bad for you to be outside so much. It will make your rheumatism worse."

"Oh, it's spring now," said Dick. "It's not cold any more. I feel hot when I'm outside with my jacket on."

"The doctor said you must take plenty of rest," said Mom.

"He was just babying me, Mom," said Dick. "Besides, I had a good rest today. I've been lying down on the couch ever since supper."

Mom turned to Dad. "What do you think, Mark?"

Dick looked at Dad too. Would Dad tell about the tumble from the tractor? If he did, it meant bed sure for Dick. Dad looked up from his paper.

"This is no child's play, son," he said. "Farrowing is a serious business and hard work. I don't want to lose any little pigs this year. I want to save them all this time."

"I've tamed Susie," said Dick. "If I'm there, she'll be easier to handle. She won't get so excited."

Dad thought for a minute, then he said, "If you'll stay out of the way and not bother us, you can watch for a while. But don't go getting sleepy on me. I'll have no time to bother with you."

It was quite late when Mark Hoffman and Dick went to the hog-house. Raymond returned from the Rudens' and came out to help. The hog-house was a busy place. Dick perched up on a bale of straw in the alleyway to watch.

It was dark now outside. The building was lighted with a few dim overhead lights. Everything began to happen at once. Dad and Raymond kept going back and forth, caring for the sows, but Dick stayed close by Susie. He rubbed her ears and scratched her back to keep her quiet. Then Dad came back to help Susie. He got down on his knees and used straw and a gunny sack to rub the wet new pigs off as soon as they were farrowed. Then he pushed them over under the heat lamp in the corner of the pen. Dick knew they must not be allowed to get cold or they would die. He lost count of how many there were. He wondered how late it was.

"Here's a little fellow that will never make it," said Dad. "He'll be a squealer. We won't waste any time on him."

Dick picked up the runty pig and wrapped it in a sack. When Mom came out, she saw Dick curled up on the bale of straw fast asleep.

"Take that boy out of here," said Dad.

Mom shook Dick by the shoulder to waken him. Dick heard a voice telling him to go to the house. He cuddled the little runt in his arms and stumbled out the door. The barnyard looked strange. It must be midnight now. He had never been up so late before. The bright electric yard-light on top of the tall pole, brightened everything, but threw strange dark shadows behind the circle of farm buildings. They made it look like somebody else's barnyard, not the familiar one that Dick knew so well. The last thing he remembered was putting the little runt in a box behind the range. Mom spooned some milk down the pig's throat. The kitchen was warm and Dick knew it would be safe there.

The next morning Dick slept late. When he came down for breakfast, Dad's and Raymond's places were empty.

Excited, Dick asked his mother: "How many pigs? How many

did Susie have? Where are Dad and Raymond?"

"Still sleeping," said Mom. "They were up and down all night. Dad said for you to go out and water Susie and the other sows. See that Susie doesn't lie on her pigs and crush them. Give her water and a little mash—not much."

Dick did not wait to eat breakfast. He and Margy ran out to the hog-house.

"Don't talk loud," said Dick, "and be sure to move easy. Any sharp noise or move will make a sow jump up and step on her pigs."

The two children tiptoed in. The little pigs in Susie's pen were nursing contentedly. Dick counted and there were eleven.

"Eleven! Not counting the runt."

"Oh, how cute they are," said Margy. "I want one."

"Wait till you see my runt," said Dick.

After bringing feed and water for the sows, and looking in the other pens, Dick and Margy decided that Susie's pigs were the nicest. The children ran back to the kitchen to see the runt. It was still alive. Dick warmed a little diluted milk and fed it from a spoon first.

"Let me hold it," cried Margy. "Can't I feed it?"

"No," said Dick. "It's too little."

"You can take that pig right back to its mother," said Mom.

"Aw, Mom—I want to make a pet out of it," said Dick. "I know just how to raise it. I read up on it in the farm magazine. I have to give it warm milk every two hours."

"Out of a bottle, like a baby?" asked Margy.

"No," said Dick. "Pigs don't drink out of bottles like baby lambs. It will soon stand up and drink out of a pie pan, you'll see."

"Not one of my pie pans," said Mom. "Take it out to its mother and let it nurse."

"It's too little," said Dick. "Those other eleven big ones will never let it get anything to eat."

Dick coaxed, and at last Mom said: "Well, only for a day or two. Then out it goes."

Margy looked at Dick. "What's its name?"

The little runt made a noise.

"Squeaky," said Dick.

CHAPTER II

A Bird in Hand

"What you kids up to?" called Dad.

Dad heard a loud commotion—dog barking, chickens squawking, geese running and flapping their wings. Around the corner of the barn came Dick and Margy riding on a cow's back. It was Flossie, one of the milk cows. A bridle and harness had been rigged out of ropes. Elmer Ruden had come over to play. Elmer was plump and short and had a butch hair cut. He walked behind and held the reins. When he slapped Flossie with his whip, she kicked up her heels and Margy squealed.

"We're breaking Flossie to ride," answered Dick.

"You'll be breaking your necks," said Dad, "if you don't watch out. **Better** go put that cow back in the pasture where she belongs. Then come back here and help me, boys."

Dick slid off Flossie's back and helped Margy down. He took the cow's harness off. He opened the gate and let her into the pasture. Margy ran to the house. Dick and Elmer helped Dad pull the corn planter out from the shed. Dad took it out in two pieces. The corn planter had to be pulled by the tractor. It had four round boxes on it, into which the seed corn was poured. It planted four rows at a time. Planting proceeded as fast as the tractor could be driven in loose dirt.

"Going to plant corn, Dad?" asked Dick.

"Sure," said Dad, "if it don't rain."

He told Dick to get some boards. Dick put them under the sharp pieces that make the rows. Dick brought grease-can and toolbox from the tool shed. Dad used bolts and nuts to set the machine together. He greased it in a number of places. He tried kernels of corn between the plates. He worked for an hour, while the boys watched.

"When the kernels go through real nice," Dad said, "it's all set to plant corn."

"How long before the corn comes up, Dad?" asked Dick.

"It'll be up in seven days of good weather."

Dick turned to Elmer. "Here it's the first week of May already and the corn's not in. It's taken so long to get the fields ready. First you plow, then disc, then drag, then plant, then drag. The reason you have to drag so much is to keep the ground level. Raymond said if you didn't, you would break the cultivator."

"What would I care?" laughed Elmer. "Then I'd ride to town and get it fixed."

"But the important thing is to get the crop in before it rains," Dick went on.

All the neighbors grew corn as their major crop. Some had finished planting the week before. Dick was as concerned as his father over the delay and the prospects for a good crop.

"Don't worry, Dick," said Dad. "All we can do is plant the corn. Then hope and pray that we'll get enough rain to make it grow, that the hail won't ruin it, that the bugs and corn borers will let it alone, that it doesn't get drowned out by too much rain or dried up in the hot sun. Then maybe, we'll have a good crop."

The boys laughed. Dad attached the planter to the new tractor. He loaded two sacks of hybrid corn on.

"Can I drive for you, Dad?" asked Dick.

"No," said Dad. "I don't want to land in the ditch. Listen now, Dick. When Raymond and I are busy in the field, plowing and planting, remember you are in charge of things around here. Don't do anything foolish. If we don't get in by chore time, you'll have the chores to do."

"Wilma will help me," said Dick. "If she helps, she won't have to wash dishes."

As his father drove out the lane, Dick's eyes followed the new tractor with longing. When would he ever be allowed to drive it?

"Let's do something," said Elmer Ruden.

"Want to see a crow's nest?" asked Dick.

"Sure," said Elmer. "Where is it?"

"Oh—somewhere," said Dick, cautiously. "Let's go over to the grove."

Two double rows of trees—Chinese elms, mulberries and box elders—had been planted on the northwest side of the homestead

[16]

to act as windbreak and snow-catcher. The region had formerly been prairie land, treeless, virgin prairie grass. Only the toughest trees would grow. Every grove in the region meant shelter for a farm home and buildings.

At one edge of the grove was the farm junk yard. Here old iron, tin cans, tires, wire and discarded machinery had been piled. Elmer and Dick began prowling, when Margy turned up.

"Margy!" scolded Dick. "Go back in the house. You can't come with us."

Margy turned back whimpering. "I'll tell Mama on you."

"Where's that crow's nest?" demanded Elmer.

"It's up in the tiptop of a pine tree," said Dick. "It's got some baby crows in it, too. They're getting feathers already."

"Let's catch them," said Elmer.

"What for?" asked Dick, with a serious look on his face.

"I'd like one for a pet," said Elmer. "If you slit their tongues, you can teach them to talk."

"You just want to hurt them," said Dick. "I know *you*."

Dick started back toward the barnyard.

"Where's that pine tree?" Elmer kept asking. "Where's that crow's nest?"

"I won't show you now," said Dick. "I've changed my mind."

They walked past his mother's vegetable garden. Dick pointed. "See our raspberries—they're not blooming yet. New sprouts are growing out of the old ones. If they keep on like that, we'll have to move the fence over."

Elmer scowled. "Where's that crow's nest?" he demanded.

Dick walked on. As they passed the mulberry bush, several goldfinches flew out.

"My mother says this bush is bird-heaven," said Dick, "because the birds like it so much. They nest here in the spring and they come in the summer to get berries to eat." A bird flew overhead. "Do you know that bird?" Dick went on. "That was a brown thrasher." Then he felt like kicking himself. He knew he must not talk about birds to Elmer.

"I wish I'd brought my BB gun," said Elmer. "You got so many birds around here . . ."

Dick closed his lips tight. He looked at the newly planted vegetable rows in the garden. He tried to think of something to say. "Mom's lettuce will soon be up," he said lamely.

But Elmer was not listening. He had spotted a bird's nest in a pear tree.

"I see a bird's nest," said Elmer. "I'll get it before you do."

Dick looked up and saw it too. It was a yellow-breasted fly-catcher's nest. There was one baby bird in it—the others must have flown. Dick's face turned white.

"Let's rob it," said Elmer. "I'm collecting bird's eggs."

"There are no eggs in it," said Dick. "They're all hatched out."

Elmer was quicker than Dick. He was halfway up the tree already. Dick was trembling all over.

"I'll get the bird then," said Elmer.

"What do you want it for?" cried Dick. "Let it alone—it won't hurt you any. Let it alone, I say."

"You can keep your old crow's nest," said Elmer. "I saw this one first and it's mine."

Elmer slid down the tree with the baby bird in his fist.

" 'A bird in hand," he quoted, " 'is worth two in the bush.' See, I've got it!"

[18]

Then he staggered back, so surprised he did not know what had hit him. Dick's action was quite unexpected. His fist had shot out and slugged Elmer right in the face.

"Turn that bird loose!" cried Dick in an angry voice.

The suddenness of the blow made Elmer drop the bird. It fluttered on the ground. Dick ran and picked it up. He put it inside his shirt, just above his belt. He could feel it warm and fluttering, against his undershirt.

Elmer stared at him.

"You go on," said Dick. "Go round the corner of the barn and wait for me there."

"What you gonna do with *my bird*?" asked Elmer.

"It's not *your* bird," said Dick. "It's *mine* now. I won't kill it like you intended to."

Dick waited until Elmer was out of sight. Then he climbed up and put the bird back in the nest.

"Fly away soon, little bird," he said, "and then you'll be safe."

Dick went over where Elmer was waiting. He walked up to Elmer and said, "I can do something nobody else can do."

Elmer looked up in surprise. Dick was not in the habit of bragging.

"What? Tell me. Bet I can do it too."

"I can ride a hog!" said Dick.

Elmer shouted with laughter. Here was something new to tease Dick about. He liked making fun of Dick. "Show me," he said.

The boys made their way to the hog lot. They heard voices up by the house and saw the girls. Elmer's sister Donna, aged thirteen, had come over to visit Wilma.

"Come on down and ride a pig!" called Elmer.

Wilma and Donna came on the run, with Margy following.

"Don't be a tag-along sister, Margy," scolded Wilma. "Why do you have to go everywhere I go?"

"I can do all the things you big girls do," replied Margy.

Dick opened the gate and they all went into the hog lot. The hogs ran off to the far corner. They began to scratch their back on the fence posts.

"Grandma's the best one to ride," said Dick.

He went over to get her and soon Grandma came lumbering up—an oversized Yorkshire, dirty white in color. She was caked with wet and dry mud from wallowing. She snorted and grunted.

"I named her Grandma," said Wilma, "because she's so old and grouchy. She's so old she's got three wrinkles across her nose. And look at those nasty little tusks coming out of her mouth! Yah!"

"She acts like she's blind," said Donna.

"Hogs have got to raise their heads to look up at you," said Wilma. "They always miss the hole they're supposed to go in. Their eyes are fixed to look down."

"Their ears cover up their eyes too," said Donna. "No wonder they never know where they are going."

Dick brought Grandma up closer.

"You're not going to ride *her,* are you, Dick?" asked Donna.

"Oh sure," said Dick. "Grandma's a great pet of mine."

"You don't mean *her?*" said Elmer.

"I sure do," said Dick. "If I ride her and stick on, will you promise to do it, too?"

Elmer looked scared. He hedged. "I'll bet a dollar you'll fall off," he said.

[20]

Dick scratched the hog behind her ears. Then he jumped on her back. He had ridden her quite a few times before, so she was used to him. It was not easy to stay on a pig's back because of its short hair. Dick put his knees up tight against her sides, leaning over low. He rode around the lot, guiding Grandma with gentle slaps on the side of her head.

The girls cheered. Even Elmer shouted with delight.

"Your turn now, Elmer!" cried Dick, jumping off.

"Let's let the girls try it," said Elmer. "You're next, Wilma."

Wilma and Donna laughed and were game. But they did not get far. Their legs were too long and dragged. They could not hold on tight. They tumbled off on the ground and got up laughing.

"*My* turn now!" cried Margy eagerly.

"Oh, you're a baby," said Wilma. "You can't ride."

Margy stamped her foot. "I'm *not* a baby! I'm a big girl!"

"Your turn now, Elmer," said Dick again.

Grandma was over by the wagon, eating corn. Elmer climbed up on the wagon, then jumped off and landed with a jolt on the hog's back. The hog was surprised and started off squealing. Elmer yipped at the top of his voice. Suddenly Grandma turned and started back. Elmer was not ready for turning and fell off to the ground. He got up, rubbing his head. He leaned over, rubbing his leg.

"Gee, that was no fun," he said.

"You didn't hurt yourself, did you?" asked Dick.

Elmer refused to answer. The boys and girls walked slowly out of the lot. After Dick fastened the gate, he saw Elmer and Donna going off down the lane.

"He's not sore, is he?" Dick asked Wilma.

"Well, if he is, he'll get over it," said Wilma.

When they went in the house, Mom called: "Dick, you'll have to take this runt out of the house. I've had it in here long enough. I'm tired of it."

"Aw—shoot!" said Dick. "Don't call it a runt. Its name is Squeaky."

"Remember you've got the chores to do," Mom went on. "Dad and Raymond won't be in from the field till late tonight. Margy, you go gather the eggs."

Dick knew he could not keep Squeaky in the house forever. So he and Margy carried the little pig out in its box. Wilma followed.

"I'll do the chicken chores, Dick," said Wilma, "if you'll do the pig chores. Then we'll all bring in the cows and Mom will come and help us with the milking. Margy can gather the eggs."

"O. K.," said Dick. He was glad Wilma liked to help. She enjoyed outdoor work better than housework. Dick liked the pig chores, because he liked pigs better than chickens. The chore he hated most was gathering eggs.

Dick and Margy set Squeaky's box down in the alleyway of the hog-house. Margy brought a pan of milk. The little pig tipped it over, so she had to get some more.

"We'll soon be feeding Squeaky shelled corn and pig pellets," said Dick. "Then she'll grow fast."

Suddenly the boy heard some one calling.

"Dick! Dick! Come here right away!" It was Wilma's voice.

"Go and see where she is, Margy," said Dick.

Margy ran out and soon came back.

"Wilma's cornered in the barn and can't get out," said Margy. "She told me not to come in, because the mother pig is mean. It's too dangerous. She might take after me."

"Oh, heck!" cried Dick. "Now, what next?"

Dick ran out. "You go back to the house and stay with Mom, Margy," he called.

Margy scuttled away.

One glance inside the barn door showed Dick what the trouble was. Wilma had come in the barn to get chicken feed and had been cornered by an old sow and her little ones. Dick looked. It was the one he had named Lady. Wilma was hanging halfway up the hayloft ladder. She did not want to go up and she was afraid to come down. She could not get past the pig below.

"Lady's not supposed to be in here," said Dick.

"She wanted to make her nest here in the straw," said Wilma.

"We'll have to move her to the hog-house," said Dick, "and it won't be an easy job. Wait till I get a bushel basket."

"Get me down!" cried Wilma. "Get me down!"

"Give me time," said Dick.

The boy ran to find a basket and filled it half full of straw. It took a lot of courage to pick up the little pigs. He picked up the first two. Lady turned from the ladder and grunted at him. Dick scratched her on the back.

"Now you get down slowly, Wilma," he said, "and pick up the others and put them in the basket. I'll keep rubbing Lady."

Wilma did as she was told.

"Now go open the door," said Dick. "You go out first. I'll bring the basket and see if she'll follow me over to the hog-house."

But Lady did not come. Dick set the basket down and came

back with a board. Wilma brought a stick to help. Dick got behind the sow and hit her a little to keep her going. Lady refused to move, so he climbed up on a partition and prodded her with his foot. Wilma touched her lightly with her stick. These motions got her started. But she headed in the wrong direction—right toward Wilma.

"She's got it *in* for me!" cried Wilma, frightened. "She's coming after me!"

"Don't act scared," said Dick. "Hold your ground. Tap her on the nose with your stick to turn her around."

It was easier said than done. By careful coaxing, the boy and girl got the pig started in the direction of the hog-house. Dick ran ahead and brought the basket with the little pigs in it. The pigs were squealing, so the sow followed. Dick and Wilma kept on walking to the hog-house. Here Dick had a pen ready and the door into it stood open. He emptied the little pigs out.

Lady made sure they were all there. She smelled them, snorted a little and lay down. Most of the little ones wandered off, but one was under the sow, so Dick kicked her over. He picked up the little one, and that made Lady mad again. She started after Dick. He jumped out of the pen and closed the gate quickly. He looked the little pig over.

"She's mashed it," said Wilma, coming close.

"No," said Dick, "but she's hurt its leg. It can't walk."

He set it down. The little pig tumbled over in the straw. Each time he helped it get up, it fell down again.

"It's the left front leg," said Dick. "I'll put a splint on it."

"Oh, you can't put a splint on a *baby pig*!" laughed Wilma.

"Who says I can't?" replied Dick.

The boy found a piece of slat and whittled it down to the right size. He reached in his pocket for his handkerchief. He usually carried a clean one for emergencies like this. He ripped off a strip and used it to bind the pig's leg to the slat.

"There! That's supposed to be a splint," said Dick. He put the little pig back in the pen with its mother.

"O. K., Doctor Dick!" laughed Wilma. "But I don't think it will do much good."

"We'll see," said Dick.

"Can I come in now?" called Margy at the door.

"Yes, if you'll help me with the pig chores," said Dick. "Want to get some oats for me?"

"Sure," said Margy. She took a basket and ran over to the corncrib. The oats bins were overhead. When she came back her basket was half full. She set it down.

"Look what I got!" she called.

In the basket on top of the oats lay three baby mice.

"They came down the chute with the oats," said Margy.

"They're cute," said Dick thoughtfully. "Wonder if I could tame them."

"Let's teach them tricks!" cried Margy. She clapped her hands.

Dick brought water to fill the water troughs. When he came back, he looked in the basket and said, "What did you do with your mice?"

"Oh!" said Margy, with a long face. "That mean old cat, Bob-bob, came and ate them. He gobbled them down so fast I couldn't stop him."

Dick looked out the door. "It's going to rain," he said.

He heard the tractor in the lane. Dad was coming in. He

stopped and took a good look at the little pig with the hurt leg. It was busily nursing its mother. He looked at Squeaky in the box in the alleyway. The runt was curled up in the straw, fast asleep. Dick smiled.

When chores were done, he saw that Wilma and Mom had brought the cows in and were milking. Outside, it was raining. Dad did not get much corn planted, after all. Dad had shut off the tractor motor.

"You come and cover up the planter," Dad shouted to Dick. "I've got to go back to the field and get that fertilizer off the truck. It'll get spoiled if it gets wet."

Dick pulled the canvas over the planter. He saw the tractor cushion on the tractor seat. Dad rode on a cushion to ease the jolts. He started to put it under the tractor, but decided it was too hot. He tucked it under the canvas.

A big clap of thunder hit and down came the rain. Dick and Wilma ran for the house. They stood on the back porch and watched. They saw Dad come back down the lane in the Hudson. Raymond came in from the west forty with the old tractor and the drag. It began to hail a little.

"I'll take a raincoat out to Mom," said Wilma.

CHAPTER III

Around in Circles

"Can I help today?" Dick asked.

"Do the chores first," said Dad, "and then come out in the field."

It was Saturday and Dick was glad there was no school. He dashed out to the barnyard. The cattle were mooing in the feed lot and he heard the pigs squealing. He hurried as fast as he could.

He brought a pail of water and the hogs rushed in and bumped him around. The biggest one whom he had named Mrs. Hog bumped against him and knocked him over. He jumped up quickly, only to see that the others had tipped the water over.

Dick felt like kicking them, but he held his temper for he saw Mrs. Hog looking at him. She looked so innocent, he had to laugh out loud. Maybe Mrs. Hog did it on purpose. Under the sow's big ears, he thought he saw mischief.

"I don't mind a pig playing jokes on me," Dick said aloud, "but don't let it go too far, Mrs. Hog!"

Beside the hog lot stood the corncrib, a large building with double open doors at each end and an alleyway through the center. Dick went to a small door at one side, took a shovel and scooped corn out into a metal bushel basket. He lifted it to his shoulder, carried it to the lot and dumped the corn out on top of the hogs. Mrs. Hog got the most of it.

"There! That'll fix *you!*" Dick cried, laughing.

The hogs bounced and bumped over each other in their eagerness to get to the food.

Chores done, Dick started for the big eighty. The biggest cornfield had eighty acres in it. Dick ran out the lane with Buster galumphing along at his heels. After the cold damp days of March and April, May seemed like spring. The phoebes were singing. Dick saw two squirrels fighting over an ear of corn. He saws crows flying overhead. The oats field was already green. The corn was coming up. Beautiful fresh green V-shaped plants marked neat even rows in the rich black soil. They made a circling pattern over the rolling hill. Dick picked up a clod of dirt and broke it in his hand. He liked the feel of it. How glad he was not to be cooped up in the house any more.

He hurried over to the field. Dad was there and so was Uncle Henry. Saturday was a holiday at the factory in town, so Uncle Henry had come out for the day. Raymond had taken the old tractor over to the west forty. Dad had the new tractor and was cultivating the corn for the first time. Dad slowed up.

"Dad," yelled Dick, "can I drive for a while?"

Dad could not hear. He stopped and Dick yelled again, "Can I drive?"

"Let the boy drive," said Uncle Henry. "He can't learn any younger."

Dad seemed willing. At least he made no objections. Uncle Henry patted Dick on the back.

"Of course you can drive the tractor, Dick," he said. "You'll be a big strong farmer one of these days. Cultivating is easy. Want me to show you how?"

"Yes," said Dick. "I sure do."

Uncle Henry took Dad's place and Dick jumped on beside him. Dick rode standing and they started off. Dad stood by and watched. They went around the bend and lost sight of Dad.

"Keep your eyes on the rows ahead, and follow their curve," said Uncle Henry. "When the rows get short, you keep turning…"

They were at the end of the field now, on a fairly steep slope. Uncle Henry began to turn. He backed and went ahead several times. Dick looked behind.

"Uncle Henry!" he shouted. "Don't go *around in circles.* You're turning *on the corn!*"

Uncle Henry scowled and started off in a new direction.

Dick looked behind and called out again: "Uncle Henry, where are you going? You're taking a whole row of corn out."

Uncle Henry looked back. He stopped the tractor.

"Now, where am I?" he asked. He looked worried. "Gosh! I'm lost. I don't know which way to go. Where's your Dad?"

"Up that way." Dick pointed.

"We'll head back up there then."

Uncle Henry cut across several rows and after a while came back to the place where Mark Hoffman was waiting.

"Uncle Henry got lost, Dad!" called Dick.

Uncle Henry made it all sound like a big joke. He did not tell how much corn he had plowed out.

"How did you like it?" asked Dad.

"I admit it's easier to go up and down in straight rows, Mark," said Uncle Henry. "But still, contouring helps the crop. Water can't wash the land away so easy. But—I'm a city man myself. I'll leave all this hard work to you farmers." He grinned at Dick. "It's your turn now, boy."

Dick looked at Dad, who nodded. Dick was surprised. Had Dad forgotten that first tractor tumble, or was he just giving in to Uncle Henry? Dick mounted the tractor seat and Dad gave him some instructions.

"O. K. Dick," Dad said. "Watch out for the curves."

Dick started off with Dad and Uncle Henry watching. Then they went off to another part of the field. The small triangular shovels on the cultivator turned the soft black earth, destroying weeds and leaving only the young corn plants, whose leaves, like green ribbons, waved in the wind.

Dick liked to be out in the field alone. He wished the tractor would not make so much noise, so he could hear the birds better. Dick felt happier than he had been for a long time. He began to sing and yodel and to make up songs of his own. He tried to out-shout the tractor. He saw that blackbirds and crows were following the cultivator to pick up worms. Big old Buster followed for a while, then dashed off to chase a rabbit in the oats field.

Dick began to wish the rows were straight. It was hard to steer on the winding curves. The contour idea was all Uncle Henry's. But Dad was right—it was much harder and took longer. You had to watch out every minute. On straight rows, you just went straight back and forth. You did not have to turn first one way, then another; on the outside of a curve, then on the inside.

The wind began to blow. The dirt dried fast and dust blew up in the boy's face. That made it hard for Dick to see the road ahead. He kept brushing dirt off with his sleeve. But he kept steadily on. He had to prove to the men that that first tumble meant nothing and that he could really manage a tractor. He took the turns without trouble.

After several hours had passed, Dick began to feel tired. His legs got numb from sitting still so long. The air was chilly, not

half so warm as when he started. He turned at the edge of the field and stopped the tractor. He stood up and stretched.

He looked across the rolling fields. There were four farms in this square mile, the Heiters, the Hasses, the Rudens and the Hoffmans. Dick could see a dark grove outlined against the sky. That was the Ruden place, half a mile away. Down the road, far in the distance, he saw the Ruden tractor moving. Were they cultivating, too? He wondered if Elmer was helping his father.

Buster came running back from the oats field. The dog had not caught his rabbit, after all. Dick jumped down, patted the dog and talked to him. But he knew he had better get going again. He did not want Uncle Henry or Dad to find him resting. He started the tractor and went chugging on.

Dick's legs began to hurt. Was it that old rheumatism coming back? He hoped not. He tried to keep his eyes straight ahead. The rows of corn disappeared under the tractor, one plant after another. It made him dizzy to watch them. Cultivating was not so much fun after all. You just kept on doing the same thing all day long. That was what made it tiresome.

A flock of birds flew overhead. What kind were they? Wild ducks migrating to Canada, now that spring had come?

Dick turned around to watch them pass over. The cultivator got away and plowed out a few hills of corn. He pulled the steering wheel quickly and got back on the curve again. He hoped Dad would not notice the missing hills. He shook his head to keep from getting dizzy. He began to feel sleepy. Was it fumes from the exhaust pipe?

"Gosh!" said Dick aloud. "I can't even yawn or I'll be off the contour line!"

[33]

He looked around again. He could not see the rows of green corn behind him. Was it because he was dizzy and sleepy? He rubbed his eyes with his sleeve. He looked again—but there was no corn. He stopped the tractor and went back. To his astonishment, he saw that he had plowed out about six rods of corn. What was the matter, anyhow? He was keeping in the rows in front, but plowing out the rows at the back. Dick shook his head. He could not figure it out.

"I'll go get Dad," he said. "Maybe he'll want to take over."

Leaving the tractor in the field, Dick called Buster and they walked home. Dad came back with him and so did Uncle Henry. They soon saw what was wrong. Dad did not scold at all.

"It's an easy mistake to make," said Dad. "You are on the wrong two rows. When the planter plants four rows at a time, it leaves a wider space before it plants the next four rows. You have come back on this wider space. That's why you've plowed out the corn. You go on back home," said Dad. "I'll take over now."

Two men climbed the fence and came into the field. Dick waited to see who they were. They had stopped their truck at the side of the road. One man was Charlie Ruden, Elmer's father. The other was Grandpa Shute, whose farm was on the next road south.

"In trouble?" asked Ruden.

"Oh no," said Mark Hoffman. "You men know my brother-in-law, Henry Shumaker, don't you?"

The men nodded.

"We saw you stalled here," Ruden went on. "We thought maybe you didn't know if you were coming or going."

Dick watched his Dad. He saw his lips tighten, but he did **not** say a word.

"It sure looks funny from the road," said Grandpa Shute, "to see a man cultivating on contour. I wonder what crazy ideas they'll be thinking up next."

"Looks like a man might be drunk or something—going around in circles," Ruden went on. "First he's going one way, then he finds himself way over on the other side of the field. Don't you get lost sometimes?"

Dick knew this kind of talk would make Uncle Henry mad. He saw Dad and Uncle Henry look at each other. But they made no reply.

"When I was young," said Grandpa Shute, "I learned at school that the shortest distance between two points was a straight line. But now, they seem to figger that the farther you go round, the sooner you'll get there."

"How do you like this contour business?" asked Ruden.

"Fine," said Uncle Henry. "If we hadn't terraced this year all our corn would be down in the creek now. That was a two-and-a-half-inch rain soon after we planted." As the men turned to go, he added, "Well—got anything else to say?"

Charlie Ruden spoke for both. "We just don't like that way of farming." The men walked to the road and rode off in their truck.

Dick did not realize how angry Dad was until he spoke. He turned to Uncle Henry and exploded.

"You're making me the laughing stock of the whole neighborhood, Henry Shumaker!" he shouted. "You heard what they think of me—it looks like I'm drunk! They'll all razz me to death for my funny farming."

"Let them think it's funny," said Uncle Henry, in a joking tone. "Let them laugh . . ."

"That's easy for you to say," said Dad. "It's *me* they're laughing at, not *you*. I don't know why I ever listened to you. A tenant ought to have *some* rights. You get your half of the corn, your two-fifths of the oats and cash rent for the pasture, even when I don't make a penny!"

"Now, listen, Mark," began Uncle Henry, "you know it helps the crop—"

"I've heard that before," said Dad. "You can save your breath. Next year I'm going back to straight plowing again . . ."

He jumped on the tractor, started the motor and began to move. He had to shout to be heard over the tractor's loud roar. He hurled his angry words like weapons into the air, *"Or I'll move off to another farm!"*

Dick walked slowly back to the house. He called Buster, and the big dog bouncing heavily up and down, came behind him. Dick wished his father could own his own farm, and not rent from Uncle Henry. Every time Uncle Henry came out, it made trouble. If only Uncle Henry would stay in town where he belonged. All he cared about was making more money from the farm. The farm was nothing but cattle and hogs to him. He wanted a big corn crop, to feed the cattle and hogs—and sell them to make money.

Dick hated to hear his father talk about moving away. They had lived on Uncle Henry's farm since Dick was a small boy. It was home to him. He knew every stone and fence and tree and blade of grass on the place. Yet he knew his Dad was not satisfied and that bothered him. He felt tired and worried. Suddenly he realized that his legs were aching again.

He hated to go back to the house. Mom and the girls were not there. Mrs. Loretta Haas had stopped for them and taken them to town. They would not be back until suppertime. Mom had shopping to do. Dick went in the kitchen. He saw the table covered over with a white cloth. Under the cloth was a cold dinner set out. Dad and Uncle Henry came in and ate without talking. Dick gulped down his portion and lolled on the porch couch. He watched the men go back to the field.

Dick was still thinking about the quarrel. His thoughts were like contouring cultivating—they kept going around in circles. But they were interrupted by Buster's barking. Dick looked up just in time to see a large cow go leaping over the fence. Buster was after her. It was Clover, the new cow Dad had bought at the sale the week before. She did not feel contented yet. She wanted to go back to her former home. It looked as if she were on her way! If somebody did not stop her, she'd be out in the road soon!

Dick ran after the cow and soon caught up with her. He patted her and spoke to her. "What are you doing out here, old girl?" he asked. "You'd better stay in the cow lot. You'll like it here, after you get used to us."

Clover acted excited, so Dick drove her into the barn. When he got her there, he saw what the trouble was. She had cut her milk bag in jumping the barbed-wire fence. He knew she was in pain, for she refused to stand still. What should he do? Dick was supposed to take care of things when Dad and Raymond were not there. He knew what Dad would do—call the veterinarian to come and take a look at that cut. Dick did not hesitate. He went to the telephone and put in the call.

It seemed a long time to wait for the veterinarian to come. When the car drove in, Dick saw a young man get out. It was the old Vet's son. Dick did not know him very well. He had heard that Doc Musfelt intended to retire soon, and that his son, just out of college, was taking over his practice. Dick took Doctor Emil in the barn. He told him what the trouble was.

Clover was lying down and seemed quieter now. The young veterinarian gave her a kick. "Get up!" he said. After several kicks, the cow got up. She began to move restlessly.

"You see?" said Dick. "She got cut on the barbed wire . . ."

"You don't need to tell me," said Doctor Emil. "I can see for myself. That cut's not bad. It'll heal in a day or two." The cow lay down and the veterinarian kicked her again.

"Stop kicking her!" said Dick.

The young man stared at the boy.

"The next time you let your *Dad* phone for the veterinarian," he said. "We haven't got time to get up and run each time a kid calls on the phone or each time a cow jumps a fence." He turned to go.

"You're not leaving?" gasped Dick. "You won't do anything?" He followed out the door at the man's heels.

"There's nothing to be done," said Doctor Emil.

"She's got a deep cut in her milk bag," insisted Dick. "I looked. You didn't even examine her."

The man jumped in his car and started the motor.

"Tell your father this call will cost him $5.00," Doctor Emil said. "There's a farmer over near here who lost twenty pigs last night. I've got to go see him."

[38]

After he was gone, Dick felt stunned. What should he do? He knew Clover needed attention and promptly. She was a valuable cow and if infection set in, they might lose her. There was no one there to help her but Dick. There was no one to help him decide what to do.

He remembered last summer—the time the hogs were vaccinated for cholera. He remembered the old Vet and how he, Dick, had helped him. The old Vet would not kick a cow to make her get up. He made up his mind what to do. He ran to the telephone and looked up the old Vet's house telephone number. He called and talked to Doc Musfelt himself. Just the sound of the old Vet's voice on the phone made the boy feel calm.

"I 'spect Emil was in a big rush to get over to see Ruden's hogs," said the old man. "I'll come right out. I'd like a little drive in the country. Yes, I'll bring my satchel along. I'll take care of it now—you stop worrying."

When Doc Musfelt got out of the car, Dick took him to the barn at once. Doc never once kicked Clover. He bumped her a little and gave her a shove. The feel of his hands quieted the cow. He examined the cut and helped Dick put the cow's head in the stanchion and chain her.

"That one cut is pretty bad," he said. "It goes in about to the milk canal. The other one is slight. She's a big old cow. Surprising she can jump fences."

"You gonna do something, Doc?" asked Dick.

"Sure," said the old Vet. "Sew her up."

"Can I help you, Doc?" asked Dick.

"You sure can, son."

Doc Musfelt opened his satchel, which held a small tray. He

[39]

set his equipment out. He had needles, small knives, scissors, string, salve, and little bottles of disinfectant.

"You squat down here beside me, son," he said, "and hold this tray. When I ask for something, you hand it to me. This way, you can see how it's done." He set to work.

"You won't hurt her, will you, Doc?" asked Dick.

"No," said the old Vet. "I'll put a numbing fluid into her milk bag and she won't feel a thing." He inserted a hypodermic needle. "We'll wait a few minutes now."

"Doc," asked Dick, "do you think an animal can understand what you say to it?"

"What do you mean, son?"

"I mean—if you say 'Get up!' to a cow and she don't get up, do you think you ought to start right in beating her?"

"No," said the old Vet. "Never beat an animal."

"If a cow is lying down and you just holler 'Get up!' at her, I don't believe she would get up," said Dick, "because I don't think she understands what your words mean. Now a dog would be different. A dog is kind of understanding if he knows you real good and has been around you a long time. I think a dog can understand *the words you say.*"

"Yes," said the old Vet. "A dog can understand more than a cow. Some dogs can even *think.* With a cow, you just rub 'em and pat 'em and talk to 'em, and they seem to like the touch of your hands."

"You don't have to lose your temper," Dick went on, "and beat 'em up because they don't obey your command. You don't have to take a board and beat them. They can feel pain like anything!"

"Hand me the scissors now," said the old Vet.

Dick watched him sew up the cut. It was quiet in the barn now except for the fluttering and chirping of a few sparrows up in the rafters. Clover never even flinched. She stood still through the whole proceeding.

"She stood nice and quiet, didn't she?" said Dick.

"Yes," said Doc. "She knew we were helping her."

"I like animals," said Dick, "and I like to help them. They know when you are helping them, don't they?"

"Indeed they do," said the old Vet. His eyes twinkled as he looked down at the boy, so serious and earnest.

"Sometimes you have to be kind of brutal," Dick went on, "but when it helps them, I feel I am doing the right thing."

"A good farmer takes care of his animals," said the old Vet.

Doc Musfelt picked up his satchel and Dick walked to the car with him. He patted the boy on the shoulder and said, "Maybe you'll be a veterinarian like me some day."

Dick smiled. "I'd like to be one—as good as you, Doc. Thank you for coming out. I hope it wasn't too much trouble."

"None at all," said Doc.

"What will it cost?" asked Dick. If there were two fees to pay, Dad would make a fuss.

"Nothing at all," said Doc. "I just came for the ride."

He waved his hand and was gone. Dick felt relieved and comforted inside. When the family came back, they all went out to see Clover. Dad said Dick had done the right thing. Even Uncle Henry praised him for acting promptly. That night Uncle Henry stayed for supper and Mom had banana pie for a treat. Dad did not eat his, so Dick slipped his empty plate over and ate Dad's piece, too. Dad seldom ate pie, so he did not say anything.

The boy was tired now. Right after supper he went to bed. That night Dick could not sleep. The next morning he had fever and stayed in bed. A slight touch of flu made his rheumatism worse. His knee and elbow joints were swollen. His arms and legs ached and he could get no rest. The doctor came and said he did not like the sound of his heart. He advised bed, no school, and after he got up—crutches for a while.

"He should never have done that cultivating," said Mom.

"Uncle Henry insisted he couldn't learn any younger," said Dad. "I didn't want him to do it."

"There's one thing certain," said Mom. *"Dick is not to drive the tractor again!"* Dad agreed with her.

Not even the old one? Not even the old one.

Not to drive the tractors! It was like a death sentence. Dick raged when he heard it. How could he stay off the tractor for a whole summer? Life on the farm after school was out, would be unbearable. Two tractors and not allowed to drive! Dick could not imagine a worse fate. It made him more restless and discontented. He got tired of staying in bed. He fussed and complained. He hated crutches. After he was sick last winter, he had used them for a while. But now he was determined—never again.

One evening, Dick got out of bed and stood looking out of the upstairs window. Dad had been gone all day over to the Ludwigs, helping with the haying. Dick watched and waited until Dad drove in. He saw Margy run out to meet him. He saw Dad put a bundle in the little girl's arms and he watched her hurry toward the back door. He heard Margy ask Mom for an empty box. He heard Raymond and Wilma exclaiming over something. When

[42]

Dad came in, he heard the word "surprise." He wondered what they were all up to, but he felt too tired to care. He was about to slip back into bed again, when Mom came to the bottom of the stairs and called, "Dick! Oh Dick! Come on down for a little while."

"Is it O. K., Dad?" called Dick.

"Sure," said Dad. "Come on down. We've got a surprise for you."

A surprise? What could it be?

"I bet I know," said Dick. "A bag of popcorn."

Dick slipped his dungarees on over his pajamas and came downstairs. Mom handed him his crutches and he took them. The family were all sitting around expectantly. Dad was in his usual big chair, with the newspaper propped up in front of him.

"Where's the surprise?" asked Dick. "It's not my birthday. I

don't see any surprise. Did you bring some popcorn?"

Margy could not keep the secret any longer. She tiptoed over and pointed her finger behind the newspaper which Dad pretended to be reading.

"*There* it is!" she cried.

Dad put down his paper and Dick stared open-eyed. On Dad's lap lay a little rat terrier puppy, curled up fast asleep.

"A little puppy! For *you!*" cried Margy.

The puppy was white except for his face, which was brown with a white stripe down his nose. He had a short stubby tail.

"Popcorn!" exclaimed Dick. "He's brown and white like popcorn. I'll name him Popcorn. Where did you get him, Dad?" Dick held the soft little ball in his arms now. He patted him and the puppy opened his eyes, looked up at him and sniffed.

"Over at Ludwigs," said Dad. "Martin wanted to pay me for helping him and I told him I'd rather trade work. So he said, 'I'll give you a puppy then—for the kids.' "

Dick looked at Wilma and Raymond and Margy. "Don't you other kids want him?"

They all shook their heads. "He's yours," they said.

Dick looked at Mom. "Can I keep him . . . *upstairs?*"

Mom nodded and Margy helped Dick put him to bed in the empty box, where she had made a nest of soft cloths.

"Popcorn is a nice surprise," said Dick, his eyes shining. "Thanks a lot."

He went upstairs with the box. Mom looked at Dad.

"That's better than medicine," she said.

CHAPTER IV

Doctor Dick

While Dick was getting better, the little dog Popcorn was always with him. He slept in the box in the boy's room and ate on the rug beside his bed. The puppy quickly learned to run up and down the steep stairs. He became a good watchdog. Whenever he heard someone come in the lane, he ran downstairs and barked. All the children loved him.

"You can't have him all for yourself," said Wilma one day. "We all want a part of him."

"What part?" asked Dick.

"I'll take his two ears and his head," said Wilma.

"I'll take his tail," said Raymond.

"I want his four legs," said Margy.

"I'll take what's left—his whole body," said Dick. He hugged the puppy in his arms. "So Popcorn's *my* dog, after all."

Sometimes the children nicknamed him.

"I'll call him Trixie," said Wilma.

"I'll call him Butch," said Raymond.

"I'll call him Sassy Brat," said Margy.

"And I'll call him Stubby Tail," said Dick.

As the days went on, little Popcorn's list of nicknames grew longer and longer. Sometimes he was Jiggers or Bud or PeeWee or Hot Dog or Shicklegruber or Pie Face. But it did not matter to Popcorn. He answered to them all and was the friend of everybody.

For the first week he was the center of attention. Then Raymond brought a young wild rabbit in from the field. He gave it to Dick for a pet.

Margy patted the rabbit. "I think he got lost from his mother," she said, "because he is almost skin and bones."

"We'll feed him," said Dick, "and name him Peter."

Popcorn was moved to the sun porch downstairs and Peter slept in the box in Dick's room. Dick fed him milk with an eye-dropper first. Soon he was able to nibble carrot tops. By the time Dick left his bed and came downstairs, the pet rabbit had the run of the house. He ate celery, lettuce, Cheerios and bread. Later Dick tried feeding him corn and oats, and rabbit pellets from the feed store.

School was out now. It was June and Dick went for short walks on his crutches in the warm sunshine daily. He always took Popcorn with him. Popcorn barked at the geese in the barnyard and pestered them until they took after him. The dog ran to Dick for help. Dick talked to the geese. "You'll have to make friends with Popcorn," he said.

Dick rigged up a hoop and taught the dog how to jump through it. Margy jumped through and the dog followed her. The children played circus. They all tried to keep Dick cheered up, but it was not easy. On many days he sat in the house and moped.

"Why don't you go outside in the sunshine?" asked Mom.

Dick shook his head. "Nothing to do out there," he said. "I can't drive a tractor or even ride on one. How can I help with the windrowing or the combining? A guy's *got* to be able to drive a tractor if he lives on a farm."

Mom did not argue. She knew how the boy felt and she was sorry for him. "Will you take some lunch out to the men?" she asked.

"Aw—let Margy do that," said Dick. "That's little kids' work."

"Margy's out with the big girls," said Mom. "I don't know just where they have gone."

"What do those girls have to come over here for?" asked Dick. "That silly Donna Ruden and that prissy Rita Hass."

"They've come to spend the night with Wilma," said Mom.

"To spend *the night?*" shouted Dick. "First they come to spend the day. Do they have to spend the night, too?"

"They don't *have* to," said Mom. "They *want* to. They are Wilma's friends."

"Well, I don't like them."

"That's too bad," said Mom.

"Where's that lunch?" demanded Dick. "I'll take it out just to get away from those silly girls. But not on crutches—I can walk as good as anybody. I'm not using crutches any more—hear?"

"Well, if you're sure you don't need them . . ." said Mom.

Dick wanted to go out to the oats field where the combining was going on, but at the same time he hated to go. He felt sick that he could not drive the tractor. But he could not keep away. He would go out and watch for a while. He could look at his traps on the way back. He had set traps for pocket gophers the day before. Pocket gophers could ruin an alfalfa field, and Dad wanted to get rid of them.

Popcorn scampered at his heels and big old bouncing Buster came clumping along. The warm sun felt good through Dick's thin shirt. It was really summer now. The boy made his way slowly out to the field, bag of lunch in one arm and coffeepot in the other.

A week before, the standing oats had been the color of rich gold. When Buster ran through it, his bushy black tail could be seen waving like a flag above the uncut grain. Now the grain was cut. It had been windrowed several days before. The grain was laid down in even rows to dry out slowly. It was ready to be harvested.

Across the field came the big noisy combine. Dick could not help but feel excited when he saw it and the man on top. Was it Raymond? He could not tell because of the dust. Yes, Raymond was on the combine and Dad was driving the tractor with the wagon behind it.

The cut grain slid into the front of the machine. Straw and dust poured out from the rear onto the ground. Shelled oats went into the grain hopper on the side. When the hopper was full, Dad came close with the wagon, and a shower of grain was dumped into the wagon bed.

When the men saw Dick with his large paper bag and coffee-pot, they stopped. "Lunch!" cried Raymond. "I'm starved."

"I'm ready for it," shouted Dad.

"So are we!" cried several other voices.

Dick looked up in dismay. There were those girls riding in the oats wagon. Could he never get away from them? Dick was surprised that Dad would let them ride on the oats.

"Dad, I'm going back to the tool shed to get a file," said Raymond. He grabbed a sandwich, unhitched the wagon and drove the tractor back to the barnyard.

Dad sat on the wagon tongue and Dick sat beside him. He took Popcorn on his knees. The four girls in the body of the wagon

stopped playing and asked for something to eat. Dick knew now why Mom had sent out so much lunch. Dad passed sandwiches and they all ate. Dick was hungrier that he thought.

"We had engine trouble when we started out," said Dad.

"What was the matter?" asked Dick.

Dad's eyes twinkled. "The wrens had built a nest in the engine," he said, "and did we have a time getting it out! The radiator boiled over like a fountain."

Dick laughed. Behind him, the girls began to play again. Wilma took a shovel and made mountains out of the loose grain. The other girls made big piles and messed them up. They giggled and laughed.

"I like the feel of oats running through my hands," said Margy, trying to act as old as the big girls. She poured a trickle of oats down Dick's back—until he jumped away.

"Let's make a contour farm," said Donna.

They began to lay out hills and curving valleys.

"I'll make a creek down below," said Margy. "Then we can all go in swimming."

"My sister and I rode the windrower yesterday," said Rita Hass, "and I guess it got the best of me. I didn't feel so good last night. All that machine did was rock, rock, rock."

"Rock, rock, rock," said Wilma. "I began to feel woozy when we went bumping along in this old oats wagon."

"Rock, rock, rock!" mimicked Donna. "I'll feel better after I have a drink. Anybody bring any cold drinks for a thirsty crowd? Is that coffee?"

"No," said Dick. "It's iced tea." He poured tea from the coffee-pot into paper cups.

Margy said, "Oh, how thirsty I am." She climbed down over the wheel and picked oats straws for everybody. "Get down and have a drink, you kids."

The girls climbed down.

"Here," said Margy, "drink your tea through a straw." She passed straws out and they all drank or tried to.

"Why, heavenly days!" Wilma looked around. *"Where's Dad?"*

"He was here a minute ago," said Donna. "Remember—he passed out the sandwiches."

Margy looked under the wagon bed. The girls looked under and around the combine. They looked in the fields near by but could not find him.

"Where's Dad?" Wilma faced Dick. "You know. Tell us."

Dick grinned a sly grin, but would not answer.

"Dad's *lost!*" Margy began to whimper.

Just then a head and shoulders popped up over the sides of the wagon bed. There was Dad. He had climbed inside the wagon to level off the oats. The girls shrieked with laughter.

Dad was waiting for Raymond to came back with the tractor. The girls kept on playing and laughing. They waited to ride back on the oats wagon.

Dick gave the coffeepot to Wilma and walked off. It was fun to be outdoors. He walked over by the alfalfa field to see about his gopher traps. He hated to kill animals, but when they were pests and ruined a crop, there was no choice. To get all the gophers out of a field, he knew he should have a dozen traps or more. He owned only two, so could set only two at a time.

In making their tunnels, the gophers push out excess dirt into a

[51]

mound. Then they plug up the hole. Dick found one of the mounds. He dug down to the place where the tunnel forked and found his first trap. There was nothing in it. But in the second trap, something was alive and moving. Was it a gopher caught by the leg? It had stripes down its back. It was a chipmunk, not a pocket gopher.

Dick looked more closely. There had been rain the night before. The hole in which the trap was set had filled with water and the poor chipmunk was half-drowned. Dick took it out of the trap and wrapped it up in his ever-ready handkerchief, even though its leg was bloody. The little animal was almost dead from lack of blood. He tucked it inside the front of his shirt, just above his belt. He started off toward home.

He wondered where Popcorn was, so he whistled and called. Soon Popcorn came tearing along at his heels.

There was no one at the barnyard. Everything was quiet except for the contented noises of the animals. Dick lighted a heat-lamp and, wrapping the chipmunk in an old sack, placed it under the lamp. He hurried to the house. The kitchen was empty, too. He did not see or hear the girls anywhere. Mom was gone. This made it easier for him to get the equipment he needed. When he returned to the barn, the chipmunk looked better. It had more life in it and opened its eyes. Dick examined it. Its leg was broken and swollen. He thought it had best be taken off. He tied a string around the animal's leg to shut off the nerves. He waited until it got numb. Then he took a sharp knife, which he had sterilized in the kitchen and cut the leg off above where it was swollen. He left enough skin over the hole for it to heal over. He put All-Purpose Salve on it and wrapped it in gauze.

[52]

Chippy struggled a little bit. Dick took the string off right away and put him under the heat-lamp again. Then he fixed a box. He put straw in the bottom and stretched chicken wire over the top. He put the chipmunk in the box. Faced with the problem of feeding him, he soon found a nest of sparrow eggs and stole one. Sparrows were pests to be got rid of. He pried the chipmunk's mouth open and poured the egg in. The animal swallowed it. Dick left a little corn, oats and alfalfa close by. Then he went out and left Chippy.

In the barnyard he saw that nobody had come. After a while, he went back in again. Part of the corn and alfalfa had been eaten, but not the oats. The chipmunk could move now. He started to tell Dick something. He had a saucy little chatter. Dick listened. It was a kind of trill really. Dick felt better. The chipmunk was going to get well.

"You should stay away from gopher traps," he told Chippy. "I'm sorry I had to hurt you, but your leg will heal quicker now."

Dick heard voices and the dogs' barking. A tractor came into the barnyard. He looked out and had a surprise. There was Mom driving, bringing in the wagonload of oats. She had a checked blouse and her slacks on. She wore a big straw hat. Raymond must have coaxed her out. Mom liked to go outdoors, but did not get the chance very often. She liked to brag about how strong she had been as a young woman. She could carry a bushel basket of oats on her shoulder; she could milk twenty cows.

The girls jumped off the oats wagon.

Dick decided he would not show them his new pet. He would not even tell them about Chippy. Yes—Chippy was a good name. He went back in and looked at his new pet. He decided Chippy was still too weak to have visitors. Margy came in for a minute.

"Hey, punkin," Dick called. Before he knew it, he had told her.

"How do you know what to feed it?" asked Margy.

"I just guess at it," said Dick. "I just follow my own notions."

But Margy was not interested. She ran out again. Dick could hear the girls playing on the loading chute. They climbed over the sides, up through them and jumped off the high end. Both dogs, Buster and Popcorn, jumped with them. The girls laughed and squealed as they jumped.

"They're worse than pigs," said Dick to himself, "the way they squeal."

Dick remembered the sows going up the chute. Last week, after the young pigs had been weaned, Dad had sold the sows. They were all gone now—Susie and Grandma and Lady and Spotty and Mrs. Hog and the other unnamed ones. Dick had watched the men prodding them with poles and electric buzzers up this same loading chute and into the waiting truck. He had hated to see them go, knowing only too well their destination— the stockyard. They would soon be ham and bacon on breakfast tables all over the country.

Dick felt sick at the thought. Mom never guessed why he had stopped eating bacon for breakfast so suddenly. Dick could not tell anybody that he was homesick and lonesome for the old sows. How the kids would razz him if they knew! Nobody liked hogs— really *liked* them and tried to understand them as he did. Everybody made fun of them, or thought of them in terms of weight and dollars. Dick puzzled about this. A hog could not help its shape or its habits. Why did it have to go through life the butt of jokes? Why was not a pig or a hog as good as any other animal?

Why should it not receive the same care and understanding? Why was a hog always an outcast?

Dick heard the girls. They were in the hog lot now. What were they doing? Starting the chores? Not likely. Was Margy showing them the runt, Squeaky? Nobody but Dick could tell Squeaky from the other pigs now, she had grown so large. The boy heard giggles and laughter and loud screams from the girls. He heard the pigs squealing. What *were* they doing? Dick strolled out.

The pigs had been chased off to the farthest corner of the lot. There they were scratching their backs against the fence posts. Beside the hog-house, on the cement feeding floor, the girls were roller skating. They had only one pair of roller skates for the four of them. Donna Ruden had brought hers over. Donna and Wilma each had one roller skate on one foot. The other foot skated on two dried corncobs. Rita Hass and Margy were using two dried corncobs under each foot. It was fun. They placed a long row of cobs four inches apart, then, with arms outspread, started skating on them. The cobs rolled under their feet like rollers under a moving house and had to be constantly replaced. The girls fell often and jumped up laughing.

"I can ride as fast as they roll!" called Rita.

Before he knew it, Dick was laughing. He went to the barn and got out Raymond's old stilts. He would have some fun too. He came out on the stilts and surprised the girls by walking across the hog lot.

"See my new crutches!" he cried.

The girls laughed. Rita now had a red rubber ball that she was tossing to Popcorn. Dick went after the ball and gave it a side-swipe with his stilt whenever he could. At last he had a tumble.

He fell on the rough thick bed of dry corncobs that covered the hog lot.

Wilma came running to see if he was hurt. But he got up, brushed himself off and said, "I've got to go see my chipmunk."

"Your *what?*" cried Wilma. "You got a new pet, Dick?"

"Yes, he has," piped up Margy, "and its name is Chippy."

"Oh you, shut up, Sassy Brat!" scolded Dick.

"Are you talking to me or to Popcorn?" retorted Margy.

"To you, and you know it," said Dick. "Guess what I did!"

All four girls were listening now.

"I amputated a chipmunk's leg."

"You did?" cried Donna. "Oh, I don't believe you. Why didn't you let me watch?"

"Gee," said Rita. "He talks just like a doctor."

" 'Doctor Dick'! That's his nickname," said Wilma.

"Hey, Doctor Dick," demanded Rita. "You going to be a horse doctor?"

"I would be if there were a few horses around," said Dick. "I'd rather doctor horses than machines. Come and I'll show you my new pet."

"Oh, I don't want to see it," said Rita. "Is it bloody? The sight of blood turns my stomach."

Donna began to boast. "It doesn't bother me. I'm going to be a nurse when I grow up."

"And take care of horses?" asked Margy.

"No, squirt—people," said Donna.

They went in the barn and the girls crowded round. Dick opened the box and lifted Chippy up for them to see.

"Isn't he cute?" they said.

Dick was disgusted. "You girls think everything is *cute*," he said.

"Will you teach him tricks, Doctor Dick?" asked Donna.

"His leg's got to heal first," said Wilma. "Even I know that much."

"Can Chippy sleep with me?" asked Margy.

The other girls laughed.

"No," said Dick. "He's going to stay here in his box. As soon as the skin grows over his leg, I'll let him go. Chipmunks don't make good captives. He probably won't eat much in captivity. If I kept him too long, he would starve to death. It will be safe to let him go in about a week, I think. Then he can take care of himself."

"Just hear that smart Doctor Dick!" giggled Rita. "He knows

[57]

all about pets, don't he? But why bother with a pet, if you can
only keep it a week?"

That night there was great excitement at the house. The girls
cooked squaw corn for supper. They fried bacon in slices and put
in onions for flavor, then added several cans of cream-style corn.
When it was brown and sizzling hot, they served it on toast to the
family. Even Mom said it was good.

After supper, the girls had a long argument about who was to
sleep together. They changed the arrangement several times. Finally it was settled that Wilma and Donna would sleep on the
floor downstairs instead of the folding couch on the porch. The
floor was more fun! Margy and Rita would sleep in the girls' bed
upstairs. Wilma set the alarm clock to go off at midnight, when
they were all to get up and exchange places.

Mom and Dad and Raymond and Dick went to bed at the
usual time. So did the girls, but not to sleep. There was a great
deal of giggling and running around in bare feet. After Dad
called out several times, the girls quieted down. But the alarm
never went off at midnight, so they did not waken. Early the next
morning, the girls on the floor downstairs heard a noise. Wilma
got up and tiptoed into the kitchen.

"Come here, Donna," she cried. "It's Peter Rabbit—he's in the
breadbox." Donna came to see.

Wilma got the rabbit out and Peter went hip-hopping across
the linoleum floor. The girls went back to bed. Donna felt something at her feet—and there was Peter. The girls took him in bed
with them and his soft fur tickled their stomachs. They giggled.

Upstairs Rita heard the giggling. She pinched Margy and
asked, "Are you awake?"

"Ye-s," said Margy in a sleepy voice, half-awake.

"Hear those kids laughing down there?" asked Rita. "I want to find out what's going on."

Rita sneaked down the stairs and Margy followed.

"It's Peter!" cried Rita. "He's in bed with them."

The rabbit jumped out of the bed. Margy ran and caught him. With Peter in her arms, she ran up the stairs. Rita came behind her. The girls below made a fuss because their pet was taken away. Upstairs Margy and Rita took Peter in their bed, but he would not stay there. He hopped out into the hall. Just then they heard a door snap shut.

They went to look, but could not find the rabbit anywhere. They even looked in the hall closet, but he wasn't there. The girls downstairs did not have him either. Peter was gone.

"I know where he is," said Margy. "He's in the boys' room. Dick's got him. Every pet I get, Dick always steals it."

Rita and Margy pounded on Dick's door.

"O. K., Doctor Dick!" they cried "We'll get even with you."

Just then Mom came to the bottom of the stairs and called, "Breakfast is ready, everybody!"

CHAPTER V

Picnic in the Grove

"Mom!" shouted Dick. "Here comes the grocery truck!"
"Help me get the eggs out, Dick," said Mom.

Dick and his mother brought several cases of fresh eggs up
from the cellar and took them out by the house-yard gate. The
grocery truck drove in. It came once a week and was driven by
two young men, Arlo and Leo Kibler, from a neighboring town.
Mom did most of her trading with them, because she could not
drive a car and go to town regularly.

"Hi, fellas!" cried Dick.

Arlo and Leo jumped down from the cab and opened up the
three big doors on the side of the truck. The inside of the doors

was lined with racks for groceries. On the roof of the truck were large square salt blocks for cattle, and an array of striped watermelons. Behind the cab was a refrigerated cabinet where perishables were carried.

"Buy me candy! Buy me an orange! Buy me an apple!" cried Margy.

"Run and get my vinegar jug, Dick," said Mom.

Mrs. Hoffman looked over the groceries and picked out what she needed—spices, dried beans, lemons, rice, flour and canned goods. Leo counted the eggs she wanted to trade and figured out the cash she owed to settle the balance. Dick held up the gallon vinegar jug at the spigot of the four-foot vinegar barrel in the rear, while Arlo siphoned it off.

But Mom and Leo were looking over the watermelons. Leo picked out two large ones and guaranteed them ripe and sweet.

"For the picnic!" cried Dick. "Gee, you boys came just in time."

Dick carried the watermelons to the cellar, while Mom and Margy took the groceries in the house. The grocery truck drove off to other farms down the road.

That night it was very hot and close, so no one slept much. As early as four-thirty in the morning the sun was shining brightly. Dad came to the foot of the stairs at five-thirty and called, "Dick! Raymond! Time to get up." Dick shook himself awake and went out to help Raymond do the milking, while Dad did the morning chores. Popcorn ran up and down the stairs, barking loudly and waking everybody up.

"Oh, I'm so happy!" Margy went dancing around in her nightgown. "Today's the day of the picnic!"

"Go back upstairs and get dressed, Margy," scolded Mom.

It was the Fourth of July. Uncle Henry and Aunt Etta and their children had come the evening before. Betsy and Patsy were twins, thirteen, Earl was nine and Denny three. They were to stay two days and two nights because Uncle Henry was taking his vacation. Mom put Uncle Henry and Aunt Etta on the folding cot on the porch, the twins took the boys' bed upstairs, and the boys had to sleep on the floor in the upper hall.

All morning everybody was bustling around, getting ready for the picnic. It was to be held in the only shady place—the grove. Mom made four pies—two pumpkin and two lemon. Wilma boiled potatoes and made potato salad. She helped Mom get all the other things ready. Betsy and Patsy tried to help, but were always in the way. Margy took Earl and Denny outside and played with them.

About half-past eleven, Dad told Raymond to get the fire ready. "Make a good one," he said.

Raymond went in the grove and with Earl's help brought out armfuls of brush. He started the fire with old dead grass. He piled small brush on the grass, then put larger pieces on top. He tried to light it, but it did not even catch. Dick came out to look.

"That's not the way to do it," he said. "You laid it all wrong."

Raymond scowled. "Well—if you know it all . . ." He walked away in disgust.

Dick set to work and made the fire over. He made a small fire that soon settled into a bed of coals, just right for roasting wieners. The girls brought the little old dinner table from the wash-house.

"Oh boy!" cried Margy. "We're going to eat pretty soon."

"What we going to eat?" demanded Denny.

"Oh, wieners and pie and beans and lemon drops and potato chips and everything," said Margy.

"Gimme some!" said Denny.

"You'll have to wait till it's ready," said Margy.

The boys formed a procession and carried the kitchen chairs out. Uncle Henry brought a reclining porch chair and made himself comfortable in the shade.

"Why don't you help, Uncle Henry?" asked Margy.

"I'm too tired," said Uncle Henry. "I worked hard all week in the factory in town."

"Uncle Henry's so lazy he won't do a thing," Margy reported to her mother.

"Sh, Margy!" said Mom. "You mustn't say that."

At twelve o'clock, Wilma and Mom brought the food out. Aunt Etta and the twins helped. Then the picnic began. Dick kept the fire going, and everybody took turns holding wieners over the fire. Even Denny learned how to do it. He began roasting wieners for all the others. They crowded round the table and helped themselves to good things. It was a hot day, one of the hottest of the summer, so the shade of the trees was welcome. Flies and gnats swarmed over the food and tormented arms and legs, but nobody seemed to notice. They sat around, talked and ate. Popcorn, the rat terrier, stayed under the table all the time. Dick kept handing him pieces of wiener-sausage when no one was looking.

After Denny got tired of roasting wieners, he came back to the table. "I want a drink! I'm thirsty!" he cried. He climbed on a chair and up on the table. Reaching for the glass pitcher, he tipped it over. A stream of ice-cold brown liquid ran across the table and over the edge into Wilma's lap. She jumped up quickly.

"Oh look! On my good dress! My best Sunday dress!" she cried. A big brown stain was all over the front.

Denny slid down from the table and ran. Wilma's legs were longer than his, so she soon caught him. She gave him a good spanking. Denny cried and yelled.

Aunt Etta jumped up. "Now Wilma," she said, "if anybody whips Denny, I'm the one to do it."

"If you'd whip him a little more often," said Wilma, "he wouldn't be such a nuisance."

"*Wilma!*" Dad's stern voice called the girl's name.

Wilma turned away, shamefaced. She ran into the house and came out with her old clothes on—a checked shirt and her oldest blue jeans. Her city cousins looked at her in dismay.

"Why, it's the Fourth of July, Wilma!" said Patsy.

"It's a holiday," said Betsy. "Have you got only *one* good dress?"

Wilma did not answer. She walked away to the barn.

Mark Hoffman disappeared for a while with Dick. They went to the cellar and came back with the two ice-cold watermelons. Dad used the big butcher knife to slice them into large hunks. Everybody ate watermelon and said how good it was. They spat the black seeds out on the ground.

After the lunch was over, Dad and Uncle Henry stretched out on the grass to rest. Uncle Henry was about to fall asleep when he felt an itching on his nose. He reached up to brush off a fly and found a live bumble bee on the end of a string. The other end was in small Denny's hand. Denny dropped the string and ran away quickly. Everybody laughed.

Uncle Henry sat up abruptly and said, "Well, Mark, when are you going to get that farm?"

Dad woke up and replied, "*What* farm?"

"Oh, the one you're going to move to when you leave here."

Dick came closer to listen. Mom and Aunt Etta were exchanging recipes over by the table.

"Farms are hard to find," said Dad in a quiet voice.

"You bet they are," said Uncle Henry. "There's not many lying around loose half as good as this one."

"And machinery costs so much," Dad went on. "If I had in cash all the money I've got tied up in farm machinery, I could go out and *buy* a farm."

"No doubt you could," said Uncle Henry. "The machinery used on a farm these days costs more than the farm itself."

"The only way you can beat it," Dad went on, "is to buy the machinery in partnership with another farmer."

"Well—I paid half the cost of the combine," said Uncle Henry, "and I bought a new tractor for you to use."

"The tractor helped us out a lot this spring," said Dad amiably. "We got our corn in good and early."

The women were listening now.

"Mark gets pretty discouraged," Mrs. Hoffman said, "but I tell him that goes with farming. All you can do on a farm is to make enough money to put the crop back in again next year. It's an endless circle. We never get much ahead. There are always unexpected expenses to take the little that we save."

"It costs money to build up the soil too," said Dad. "Too much goes back into the land, but if you don't do it, you don't get a crop." He did not sound hopeful.

[65]

Aunt Etta turned to Mom: "How *can* you stand it out here, Bertha?"

"Why, we like it, Etta—the kids and I," said Mom. " 'You can take the girl out of the country, but you can't take the country out of the girl!' After mother died, I had to stay on the farm and keep house for father. You were little and pretty then, Etta. So they sent you to the city where Aunt Annie brought you up. But I stayed in the country and I've never known anything else. I'd like to be out in the fields all the time now, but the housework keeps me in."

"Well," said Dad. "The family's got to *eat!*"

"I do get out and help milk," said Mom. "The only thing I don't like is when it's awful hot and the cow's tail comes switching about my head and the flies are bad. Then I wish I was in Alaska!"

They all laughed.

"But aren't you going to give your children any advantages?" asked Aunt Etta.

Mom thought for a minute.

"There are plenty of advantages right here," she said quietly. "There is always clean fresh air, rain and bright sunshine. There are plants and animals to love and care for. Living close to nature gives you something that is missing in town. I wouldn't want to bring up my children anywhere but here." She turned to her brother-in-law. "Your farm is not perfect, Henry Shumaker, but we're as contented here as if it were our own."

Dad looked at Uncle Henry and grinned. "The missus seems to know what's best," he said.

Uncle Henry nodded. "It's *my* missus—that city girl there—

who keeps me cooped up in town. Down in my heart, I like the country better, too."

"Now, Henry," began Aunt Etta, "you know that's not true. You told me yourself you got dizzy doing that contour cultivating."

The men roared with laughter. Dick was relieved. It was funny now. The argument had faded away. Mom refused to let the holiday be spoiled. The men began to talk corn.

Ever since hybrid corn had been introduced to the corn farmers, and had begun to be generally grown, they had sung its praises. Its stalks and roots were stronger, its yield had doubled and all ears within a given field were uniformly large, the rows even and well filled. Dad spoke of the days before the corn picker was invented, when all the picking was done by hand, and the hauling by horse and wagon.

"We are machinists now," he said. "Not farmers any more. I spend far more time tinkering and repairing machinery than I do sowing, planting and reaping. Farms have turned into factories."

Dick went out to the big eighty, pulled the tallest cornstalk he could find and brought it back to show the men. He stretched his arm up to show how tall it was.

" 'Knee high,' that's nothing! It's head high by the Fourth of July," said Uncle Henry, proudly. "I never saw corn as fine as that before—"

He stopped in the middle of his sentence and looked over to the barnyard. Dad and the women looked up, too. Dick stood staring. They all heard the roar of a tractor. It was the new one— Uncle Henry's.

"Now, who on earth—" began Uncle Henry. "I told those girls they were not even to ask to ride on the new tractor."

"Where's Raymond going?" asked Dad. "I told him we'd take a few days off, now that cultivating is done and the corn is laid by. I don't know where he's going."

"It's not Raymond, Dad," said Dick.

The men jumped up and the women too.

"Whoever is driving," said Uncle Henry, "don't seem to know where they are going." He looked at Mom. "Can it be Wilma? What's she doing?" He glanced at Aunt Etta. "Patsy wouldn't have the nerve, would she?"

"It's not any of the girls," said Dick. "It's not even Earl. *It's Denny!*"

By this time they could see that the tractor was going in a large circle around the huge barnyard. They all ran toward it. Mom and Aunt Etta came too. Over at the barn door stood the girls, Wilma and the twins, Margy and Earl. Dick ran toward them yelling, "Get him off! Get him off!"

Then they saw Raymond tearing after the tractor. There was three-year-old Denny standing up, with the steering wheel firmly grasped in his small hands, trying to behave like a big man. He was smiling happily. He had turned the key on the starter, stepped on a pedal and started it all by himself. Now it was going where he wanted it to go—as easy as his own toy automobile at home. He was in perfect bliss. The tractor must have been left in gear on a downgrade, with wheels slightly turned. All Denny had to do was press the gas pedal with his foot and hold the wheel. The tractor kept right on going. He loved the loud noise it made.

[68]

"*Den*-ny! *Den*-ny!" screamed Aunt Etta, wringing her hands.

She was ready to dash out in front of the lunging machine, but Mom pulled her back.

"Don't be foolish," called Mom. "The men will stop it. The men will get him off."

"He'll hit something!" screamed Aunt Etta. "He'll be killed!"

Mom put her arms around Aunt Etta and told her not to look. Over at the barn door, the children were crying with fright. Dick ran across in front of the tractor, hoping to hop on after it passed. He narrowly escaped being hit. He had to go and lean against the barn door to get his breath. His heart was pounding. The tractor was going in bursts of speed, now faster, then slower, then faster. Denny was frightened now. He had let go of the wheel and was hanging onto the seat with both hands.

"Stand still, Denny! Don't move!" called Uncle Henry. "Daddy's coming."

Dad shouted to Raymond. It was Raymond with his long legs who got there first, leaped on from the rear and stopped the engine. The next minute, the tractor banged into the broad side of the barn. It broke the siding into splinters and went halfway in. But Denny was safe. Raymond had leaped off just in time, with the boy in his arms.

They all crowded round Denny, and, like a baby, he was passed from arm to arm. His tears were soon dried and he smiled broadly, happy to again be the center of attention.

"I can drive Daddy's new tractor, can't I, Mom?" he bragged.

Aunt Etta smothered him in kisses.

"Better give him the spanking he deserves," said Dad.

"I told you," said Uncle Henry, "these modern kids can drive

by instinct. You don't need to teach them how."

This time Dick spoke up. "But Uncle Henry, he might have killed somebody."

Dad added, "He might even have killed himself."

Wilma stalked off, disgusted. "Now Denny will be more spoiled than ever," she said.

The women and girls took Denny and went back in the grove to clear up the picnic. The men and boys stayed at the scene of the accident. Raymond backed the tractor out and they found that only one fender was bent. The chief damage was the big hole in the side of the barn. Uncle Henry said he would bring lumber to repair it the next time he came out from town.

"Dad," said Dick, "how about a game of horseshoes?"

"Fine," said Dad. "It wouldn't be Fourth of July without horseshoes. A fine old American custom."

"There's only one better," added Uncle Henry, "and that's firing firecrackers, the way we did when we were boys. But they won't let us do that any more."

"Dick," said Dad, "run and bring the horseshoes."

Dick went in the barn. Across a two-by-four beam hung a collection of old horseshoes of all sizes. On pegs at one side hung many sets of harness, now dust-covered, mute symbols of the past. Dad refused to throw any away. Dick still remembered the time about six years before when Dad sold his last team of horses. Dad refused to lead them out to the truck at the end of the lane. The man had to come in and get them. Dad went into the house so he would not have to watch them go.

Dick stopped and fingered the harness. If he could only have lived in the days of horses, he would not mind being forbidden the tractor. A horse was something alive. A person could love a horse far more than a machine. A horse had as much intelligence as a dog, a lot more than a hog. Machines had no personality at all, no understanding, no intelligence. They were dangerous.

Dick remembered the time when "the iron man" came to get the old horse-drawn machinery that was not used any more but was all lined up and rusting in the grove. Dick and Raymond had watched while the iron man tore it all down. He drove off with two big truckloads. Dad did not watch that go either.

But the men were waiting for him. Dick took the horseshoes out and the game began. The cheerful *clang, clang* of the iron horseshoes against the iron stake, the dull thud as they hit the soft ground and bounced in the dust satisfied the boy. He could play almost as well as Dad could. But Earl, his cousin, could never hit the stake at all.

That night they ate supper indoors. Afterward, the cousins went with Wilma and Dick to get the cows. Raymond and Dad did the hog chores and Earl and Margy the chicken chores.

As the children made their way to the pasture, Buster and Popcorn frisked and jumped beside them. Dick brought a handful of red apples from the kitchen. The Hasses had a tree and Mrs. Hass had sent some over. The children munched apples and threw away the cores. Then the girls began to sing and Dick to whistle. The air was cooler now as the sun began to sink lower in the west.

The cattle were waiting at the gate. Buster ran and brought up one from a distant corner. Popcorn dashed off in another direction. Dick opened the gate and they started driving the cows through. Their path led along by the creek. Wilma looked around. Behind her, the grass was tall and she saw it waving. She did not think much of it. Then she stopped to see if it was Popcorn coming. She saw a dark bushy tail waving over the grass. It was not Buster's, for Buster was in plain sight, still over in the field.

"Look!" Wilma said to Patsy. "There comes one of the cats. See its tail? It's following us."

"How many cats have you?" asked Betsy.

"Oh, about fourteen, I think," said Wilma.

"Where do you keep them?" asked Patsy.

"Bob-bob stays up at the house," said Wilma. "The others are just barn cats. They live in the barn and corncrib. They live off rats and mice."

Wilma looked around again. The tail was coming closer. It was big and bushy. Suddenly she knew.

"Dick!" screamed Wilma. "It's a *skunk!*"

"A skunk!" echoed Patsy and Betsy. Even the two city girls knew the menace of that dread word. Their eyes opened in terror.

"Run, girls, run!" cried Wilma. "It's a skunk! Dick! It's coming right *at* us."

Dick's first thought was to look for a weapon, but there was none handy. No rock, no stone or stick to pick up. The animal was moving fast. Dick had to think quickly. He knew there was something wrong with the skunk or it would not be chasing them. A well skunk, if left alone, would be frightened of people and go the other way. Dick had only his feet, his shoes, to use as weapons.

Buster returned, barking noisily and sniffing. The dog started after the skunk, then backed up, then started after it again. Each time the dog ducked back, afraid of being bitten. The skunk dodged back. When the dog received a heavy dose of skunk spray, he ran away yelping. Patsy and Betsy ran screaming toward the cows. But the cows were excited, too. The girls were afraid of the cows, so they came screaming back. They huddled together, not knowing which way to go.

Dick kicked the animal when it came near. It turned again. Dick knocked it in the creek, but the blow only stunned it. It started coming after the children. Wilma, who had stood by ready to help, took off her shoe and threw it to Dick. The boy caught the shoe and hit the animal on the head with it as hard as he could. At last it was dead.

But it had done its work. All the children had been sprayed and one of the cows. Dick and Wilma got the worst of it. The children stood around and looked at the dead animal. Then they looked at themselves. Patsy and Betsy fell into each other's arms sobbing.

Wilma said, "Heavenly days! That's nothing. Things like this happen all the time on a farm. It was *only* a skunk."

Dick took a deep breath. "Never saw a skunk behave like that in my life before."

"*Only* a skunk!" sobbed Betsy. "Just *look* at us!" She lifted up her ruffled, flowered skirt. "And *smell* us!" sobbed Patsy. "I hate your old farm, and I'm never coming out here again as long as I live."

Wilma looked down at her old shirt and ragged jeans. She was glad now she had changed. But she was too genuinely sorry for her cousins to brag about her own good luck.

"We'll have to bury all our clothes," she said quietly.

"*Bury* our clothes?" said Patsy. "What do you mean?"

"Why, these dresses are just new," sobbed Betsy. "We just bought them for the Fourth of July picnic. Can't we wash them to get the smell out?"

"Skunk smell will never come out," said Wilma.

"If we bury our clothes, what will we wear?" wailed Patsy.

"Oh!" said Wilma. "We'll dig up some old rags for you to wear back to town."

"That smell is on my hands and arms too," cried Patsy.

"And all over my legs and shoes and socks," added Betsy.

"We all have to take baths," said Wilma flatly.

"And have a good long soak," said Dick. "We know what to do. This has happened to us plenty of times. Mom has some special soap to use and a disinfectant. But even then, it takes a lot of soaking." Dick turned the animal over with his foot. "Old

Skunky, you know how to protect yourself from people all right, don't you? We wouldn't have made trouble for you if you hadn't chased us."

The cow that had been sprayed ran to the far end of the pasture. Buster could not bring her in. Dick called him and the children followed the cows. Dick picked up the skunk and carried it by the tail.

"Why do you bring that nasty old thing?" asked Patsy.

"I want Dad and Raymond to see it," said Dick. "It must have had the rabies. A good thing Buster is such a coward and wouldn't come near. If the skunk had bit him, he'd get the rabies too, and have to be killed."

"I heard Dad say the Ludwigs killed a rabid skunk last week," said Wilma. "Where's Popcorn?"

"Gone back to the house," said Dick. "I'm glad he didn't stay with us."

Dad and Raymond and Uncle Henry and Margy met the children halfway back to the barn. Dick threw the dead animal at Raymond's feet.

"What's this?" laughed Raymond. "A new pet?"

"DON'T COME NEAR US!" warned Dad.

Uncle Henry began to joke and hold his nose and tease his daughters. But they did not think it funny at all. Margy ran back to tell Mom and Aunt Etta. Aunt Etta made a great fuss while Mom built a fire in the wash-house stove to heat water for the children's baths. The clothes were buried by Dad and Uncle Henry and the wash-house was a busy place that night. As for poor old Buster, he had to spend weeks in the doghouse!

CHAPTER VI

The Lost Corn Knife

"We'll have to get after those cockleburrs," announced Dad one evening.

"*Ugh!* Cockleburrs!" All the children groaned.

It was several weeks after the Fourth of July and the picnic with its exciting ending was a thing of the past.

"A single burr when it first forms is poisonous and can kill a hog," Dad went on. "If we leave one plant, it's as bad as leaving five hundred. The seed is carried by dogs and rabbits. It will wash down a creek and scatter over a whole field. It can lie dormant for seven years and still germinate and produce a big crop."

"Don't we know it!" complained Raymond. "We've spent all our lives pulling cockleburrs, chopping them, spraying them, and they're still there—all over the cornfields."

"Not all over," said Dad cheerfully. "The west forty is pretty clean. But the south side of this eighty along the fence where it meets the hogs' clover and down by the creek, is bad. We must get them out before the burrs get ripe and seed themselves. If we don't do it, the neighbors will soon be saying, 'Old Man Green is taking over the Hoffman farm.'"

"Who is 'Old Man Green'?" asked Margy.

"That's another name for Grandpa Cockleburr," said Dad.

"When we went over to Hasses' to chop theirs out," Dick said, "Mr. Hass paid us two dollars a day and fed us a big dinner too."

"On your own farm, you don't get paid," said Dad flatly. "But I'll tell you a secret—the sweet corn is ready to pick."

"Corn-on-the-cob!" cried Wilma. "Yum! Yum! I'll chop cockleburrs if I can have about ten ears to eat for dinner."

The next morning after chores and breakfast were over, Dad called everybody to come. "It rained a little last night," he said. "The cockleburrs will pull easy."

Pulling cockleburrs was a family affair in the corn country. Mom and Wilma put on old slacks and shirts of Dad's. Mom wore a scarf around her head and Wilma an old straw hat. Margy wore Dick's old dungarees, big enough to fall off her. Dick and Raymond left shoes and socks at the house and rolled their pants up to their knees. They all started out. Both dogs went with them.

Because it was still early, it was damp and foggy out in the cornfield. The corn was up to a man's shoulder now, just beginning to tassel. The curly stiff leaves hung in curving arcs and rustled against each other. The wind began to blow the fog away. By noon it would be bright and sunny with midsummer heat— good corn-growing weather.

The family spread out at the edge of the field. Dad and Mom and Raymond took four rows each. Dick and Wilma took two,

Margy tagged along between Mom and Wilma. Most of the plants were young ones, with burrs just starting to form on the tips. They were easy to pull from the soft wet ground. When Dick or Wilma found one they could not pull, they called out, "Big one!" Dad or Raymond came over with the corn knife and chopped it out, cutting the root open so it would not grow again. They hung some of the larger plants on the cornstalks to dry them out. The smaller ones were left lying in piles in the row.

Dick hated cockleburrs and he hated getting rid of them. The cornstalks were wet, still dripping with rain from the night before. Pollen from the tassels dropped on bare necks and arms and stung them. The sharp edges of the long leaves hit Dick's face and cut it sometimes. Heavy corn in the ear bumped him on the head. The ground was so muddy it was hard to walk.

"Mom," said Wilma, "Rita Hass is going to sign up for detasseling. The Standard Seed Company is going to haul boys and girls out to their fields to detassel the hybrid corn. Rita's going and Donna Ruden is thinking about it."

"If you girls think it's going to be fun," said Raymond, "you are going to find out different."

"But they pay well," said Wilma, "and I need some new clothes for school this fall. Can I go, Mom?"

"I'll talk to Mrs. Hass about it," said Mom. "If she lets Rita go, I suppose you can, too."

"We have to sign up at the Farm Bureau office next Wednesday," said Wilma.

Dick reached up to find a tassel. "Boy, how you'll have to stretch!" he cried.

"But I'm taller than you," said Wilma. "The girls have to be

[80]

above five feet and I'm five feet two inches. You have to be four-teen, but they'll take you at twelve if you're tall enough."

"If you get much taller," said Dick, "you'll look like a corn-stalk yourself. That yellow hair of yours is just like a corn tassel."

"Mom!" called Margy. "I've lost both my rubbers. They came off in the mud."

"Dick," said Mom, "see if you can find her rubbers."

Margy had been walking in and out of the rows. She would follow one row until she found a stalk missing. Then she went through the empty place and followed another row. It was like going in and out of doors.

"When we get away from the ends," Margy went on, "I feel like I'm lost."

"You stay here by me," said Mom. "We haven't time to go off hunting for little lost girls."

By the time Dick found Margy's rubbers, her shoes had come off. Wilma and Mom had the same trouble. First they discarded rubbers because they became caked with mud and too heavy. When their shoes became caked too, they took them off and walked in bare feet. Dick ran back to the fence with all the shoes and rubbers. Dad and Raymond worked fast and got ahead.

"Hurry up, you slowpokes!" called Dad. "Let's try to keep together."

Margy stopped playing and tagged beside her mother. Dick's legs began to get tired and ache. But he kept on pulling and stayed abreast of Wilma and Mom. The rows were long and twisted in and out over the rolling hillside. The hours passed slowly.

"Sometimes I wonder what the corn is talking about," said Dick. "Do you hear that rustling, when the wind passes over the field?"

Wilma turned to Mom. "Dick believes he can *hear* the corn grow," she said, laughing.

"I'm not the only one," said Dick. "Scientists have *proved* it."

"What does it say, Dick?" asked Margy.

The boy frowned and bit his lips. "I know but I won't tell," he said firmly.

At last dinnertime came, so Mom and Margy went back to the house. Wilma wanted to prove how strong she was, so she went ahead with the two men. Dick found Buster covered with burrs. He led him back to the barnyard, where Margy waited. Poor Buster's shaggy hair was so covered with burrs he could not sit down. His tail was matted like a rope and Dick had to clip wads of his fur off. Then he sat down by the stock tank and patiently picked burrs out of the dog's long hair. Popcorn came up, panting.

"What are you laughing about, Stubby Tail?" asked Dick.

"Is Popcorn laughing?" asked Margy.

"Can't you see that big grin on his face?" asked Dick. "He's laughing because his hair is short and he doesn't get stuck up with cockleburrs like Buster does."

"I brought me a great big cockleburr bush from the field," said Margy. "It's all covered with burrs." She dragged a huge plant behind her.

"I'll take it and burn it," said Dick.

"No, Dick," said Margy. "Don't burn it yet."

Margy began picking the burrs off carefully. By sticking them together, she made a row of play baskets and dishes.

"See how nice they are, Dick?" she asked.

"They're nice all right," said Dick. "But you better not let Dad see you doing that. He'll stop you in a hurry."

Dick went to water the hogs and Margy followed.

"Do you remember that little runt, Squeaky?" asked Margy.

"Sure," said Dick. He pointed her out in the pen.

"Oh, that's not our Squeaky. She was a runt," said Margy. "She was little and cute."

"She grew up while you were not looking," said Dick. "I fed her so well, she grew into a big hog."

"Is she still cute?" asked Margy.

"Not very," said Dick. "Sometimes she's just plain mean, like her mother Susie used to be."

Mom came out with a bushel basket.

"I know what you're after," said Dick. "I'll bring in the sweet corn, Mom." Mom went back to the house.

The sweet corn patch was at the edge of the vegetable garden, beside the potato patch. Margy followed at Dick's heels. Dick went over to the rows.

"Look here, Margy," said Dick. "The coons have found the sweet corn already."

"How do you know?" asked Margy.

Dick pointed to the damp ground. "See their tracks?" He found a plant with empty husks hanging down from the stalk. "Old Mr. Raccoon ate his dinner right here."

"Why?" asked Margy.

"Why? Why do *you* eat? Because he was hungry," said Dick. "He likes corn-on-the-cob as much as we do. He goes right down the row, stands on his hind legs, reaches up and pulls the ears down. Then he snaps off the corn and eats it, leaving the husk hanging. The *field* corn is too tall for him to reach, that's why he comes in our *sweet* corn patch."

Margy came up closer and Dick showed her. "See the mud on this ear? His paws were muddy. He reached up, looked at this one and left it. It wasn't ripe enough to suit him. He left it for us."

Margy stared, her eyes big with wonder. "Why don't you catch Old Mr. Raccoon and have him for a pet?"

"I'd like to," said Dick. "Maybe I will some day. No, sir, people are not the only ones who like corn. Besides raccoons, woodchucks and field mice eat it, too. They depend on it. If Dad doesn't grow a big crop and spill a lot of it all over the fields, they'll go hungry this winter."

"The squirrels, too?" asked Margy.

"Yes, the squirrels eat most of all," said Dick. "I often find large piles of corncobs at the base of squirrel trees. The ground

[84]

squirrels dig the soft kernels up out of the dirt when the seed corn is sprouting in the spring. But they get the tummy ache from the bug poison and fertilizer on it!"

Margy laughed. "How do you know?"

Dick's eyes twinkled. "Statue told me so."

"Statue?" said Margy. "Who is Statue?"

"She was a mother ground squirrel I used to know," said Dick. "Once when I was taking a letter out to the mailbox for Mom, I nearly stepped on her babies. The mother sat straight up like a statue and scolded me. That's why I named her that. So I left them in their nest. I took corn and oats to them, but they liked their wild mustard seed pods best. Then winter came and they went down into their den to sleep."

"And you didn't see them any more?" asked Margy.

"In the spring they were gone," said Dick.

Dick took the basket of sweet corn into the house and he and Margy husked it. Mom had the kettle of water boiling and soon the corn was ready to eat. Dad and Raymond and Wilma came in from the field. They washed up and came in to eat. Dick sprinkled salt on the hot steaming ears, one at a time, and watched the yellow butter melt and run. He kept turning the ear as he nibbled the corn. He lost track of the number he ate.

"I'm so full of corn," he cried at last, "I feel just like Old Mr. Raccoon!"

Everybody laughed. After dinner, Dad announced that he would spray the weeds by the road. He told the boys and Wilma to go back to the cornfield.

"Can I go, too?" asked Margy.

"You can stay in with Mom, Margy," said Dad.

Dad went out the lane with his spraying outfit. The tractor pulled the sprayer with its big barrel and long hose. The last thing Dad said was, "Boys, be careful with that corn knife. Be sure you don't get cut with it."

"Come on, Dick," called Raymond.

Somehow it took the boys a long time to get started.

"Just a minute," answered Dick. "I want to see how many little chickadees there are in that nest in the apple tree." He ran out.

"You leave those green apples alone!" Mom called out of the window. "They'll make you sick. Don't eat them."

"They never made me sick yet," Dick replied, "unless it was when I was little and didn't know about it."

"Bring me in a basket of corncobs before you leave," added Mom.

Dick got his pockets full of green apples and slid down.

"There are five little chickadees up there," he told Wilma. He handed a few apples to his sister. Then he added, "The secret is to put salt on them."

"On the chickadees' tails, you mean?" asked Wilma.

"No—on the green apples, silly!" laughed Dick. "It makes them taste better and it keeps you from getting the stomachache."

"Who told you that?" asked Wilma.

"Nobody," said Dick. "I learned it myself. Here, put some salt on them. I sneaked the salt shaker out of the kitchen when Mom wasn't looking."

Wilma shook salt on hers. Raymond nibbled green apples too, and they started out. Dick stopped at the cob pile in the barn-yard and took a basketful in to his mother. Then he caught up with the others. Wilma began to spit hers out.

[86]

"They've got no taste," she said. "Those red ones Mrs. Hass uses for pies are better. They're tart and sour."

They went into the field, looking for cockleburrs. Raymond carried the corn knife. Dick and Wilma wore old gloves for pulling. All three were barefoot, with pants rolled up to their knees. They found this part of the field fairly clean, so they moved leisurely. Dick's sharp eyes were interested in all kinds of other things than cockleburrs.

He spotted a meadow lark's nest in the adjoining pasture, so he went over to look. It had one baby in it—only one, with orange-yellow fur on it. The next thing he saw was a red-winged blackbird's nest in a sour dock among the cattails at the edge of the ditch leading to the creek. The mother bird flew back and forth over his head and scolded him. So he did not go too near.

"Hey!" called Raymond. "We're not hunting birds' nests. We're chopping cockleburrs."

"Oh, but look!" cried Dick. "There's Goldie, our cow. What's she doing down here? I'm going over to see."

The next minute Dick was gone. In a short time he came running back, excited and panting.

"Goldie's had her calf," he said, "right out there near the windmill. She's in a low place by the creek where there's lots of water. If we don't take it in, the calf will die sure. It's a pretty little calf, too—what I can see of it."

Raymond hastily jabbed the corn knife into a fence post. The boys lifted the barbed wire and all three hurried over into the pasture. When Raymond saw the cow and the newborn calf, he turned to Wilma. "Run to the house and bring Dick's old wagon," he said. "Tell Mom she better come and help."

Wilma and Mom and Margy came back running. Dick had to hold the calf's nose out of the water, while Raymond got into the hole. The calf was trying to stand up in the water. At last Raymond got hold of its legs. Then Mom and Wilma and Dick all helped to lift it out and put it on some sacks in the wagon. Goldie, the mother cow, kept on mooing. Raymond pulled the calf back to the barn, where Dick put it in a stall and covered it with sacks. Mom and Wilma and Margy led Goldie mooing mournfully back to the barn. She seemed to know that they had helped her calf.

After the calf was safely cared for, Raymond said, "I'm not going out again. We got most of the cockleburrs Dad told us to get. He'll spray the others. Dick, you run out and bring in the corn knife."

"O. K.," said Dick. He returned to the creek but could not find the corn knife or remember where Raymond had left it. He saw a boy on a bicycle coming along the road. He watched him for a while. The boy stopped and left his bike by the fence. He climbed over and came in the field to see Dick.

It was Elmer Ruden. "What you doin'?" asked Elmer.

"I thought I might go down to the water hole," said Dick.

"Got any turtles there?" asked Elmer.

"Plenty," said Dick. "Bullheads and minnows, too."

"How deep is it?" asked Elmer.

"Deep enough to swim in," said Dick.

"You been swimming this summer?" asked Elmer.

"No," said Dick. He could not mention his rheumatism to Elmer or the fact that swimming was forbidden.

They started to walk, and there, right in front of him, Dick saw the corn knife sticking in a fence post. He pulled it out.

"What's that?" asked Elmer.

"Our corn knife," said Dick. "We were chopping cockleburrs this morning and left it here. I'll take it with me."

Suddenly the barking of dogs was heard. Wilma and Margy came running across the field. Buster and Popcorn came, too.

"We saw you," said Wilma. "We want to go to the creek if you kids are going."

"What's Dad doing?" asked Dick. "I saw him go back with the sprayer."

"He's starting to grind ear corn for the cattle," said Wilma. "Raymond is helping him."

"O. K. then," said Dick. "We'll go down to the water hole."

The children followed the ditch to the creek. Hogs liked to wallow at the edge and bury themselves deep in the water, with only their heads out, to keep cool. Now they all scampered away, frightened. The children came to a small bridge made of planks. They all ran over and Buster went, too. But Popcorn stopped and barked. He refused to cross.

"He's trying to tell us he's scared," said Dick. "I'll go back and get him. He can see the water through the cracks, can't you, Shicklegruber?"

Dick called and coaxed, but Popcorn would not cross. Dick picked him up and carried him over. Even in Dick's arms, the little dog held his legs stiff from fright.

"You are a little old baby," said Dick, dropping him.

Once safely across, Popcorn ran about and barked as usual. Just below the plank bridge, the creek widened into a pond about twenty feet across. The pond was always an exciting place, as it was the biggest body of water in the neighborhood. To the children, it held all the charms of lake or ocean.

"There's a fish," cried Margy. "I see a fish."

Elmer looked at Dick. "Why didn't you bring a pole?"

"Why didn't you bring one?" asked Dick. "We might catch some fish and take them home for supper."

"Where are those turtles?" asked Elmer.

"I don't know," said Dick. "Hiding, maybe."

"Why don't you dam this up," Elmer went on, "and make a real swimming hole? Can you swim?"

"I bet I can swim as good as you can," said Dick.

"We haven't any place to swim," said Wilma.

"Right here's a good place," said Elmer. "All you need to do is dam it up at this end."

"What do you know about making swimming holes?" asked Dick.

Elmer did not argue. "Let's see how deep it is here. Gimme that corn knife."

Dick handed it over. Elmer got down on his knees at the edge of the creek. He thrust the corn knife down into the water and mud. He stretched his arm down as far as he could.

"It's deeper than the corn knife and my arm," he said.

"Let me try it," said Dick.

Dick took the corn knife and plunged it in. He leaned over as far as he could.

"I'll hold your legs," said Elmer, grabbing him. "Now reach down deep."

The next minute, to everybody's surprise, Dick was *in the water*. He began to gasp and sputter and thrash his arms wildly.

[90]

"Heavenly days!" cried Wilma. "You pushed him in, Elmer Ruden. I saw you. He'll get drownded!"

Margy screamed at the top of her voice.

Elmer looked scared. He said to Wilma, "He can swim, can't he? He said he could."

"You know he can't, Elmer Ruden," said Wilma, "any more than *you* can. Nobody can learn to swim in a mudhole like this. Now you pushed him in, you can just help to pull him out."

Wilma ran, broke off the limb of a bush and came running back.

"Grab this, Dick!" She held the limb over the water and was able to pull the floating boy near the edge.

"Now, Elmer, don't stand there like a bump on a log," Wilma shouted. "Come and help pull him out. You too, Margy."

The three children leaned over and grabbed Dick's arms. He struggled in the soft mud, and they managed to pull him out.

He stood there with water and mud dripping off him.

"Well, we got you out," said Elmer, grinning. They all giggled with relief.

"What will Mom say?" asked Wilma. This was the first time any of the children had fallen in the creek. Mom had kept them scared of it since they were little. "First we pull a calf out, then Dick!" Wilma laughed.

"You can dry off in the sun, Dick," said Elmer, "and not say anything about it."

"But look at the mud on his clothes," said Wilma.

"That will dry too," said Elmer. "Then you can brush it off."

"We better go home," said Dick. His voice sounded funny.

"But don't you want to dry off first?" asked Elmer.

"Where's the corn knife?" asked Dick.

"You had it," said Elmer. "You were measuring to see how deep the water is."

"The corn knife is in the creek," said Dick. He turned on Elmer. "It was all your idea, Elmer Ruden, to measure the water. Now you can just get the corn knife out."

"Me?" said Elmer. "How can I?"

"Here, take this stick and try to find it," said Wilma.

Elmer sat down at the edge of the water. He rolled his pants leg up and stuck one foot in. He could not feel bottom and he could not find the corn knife. He lay down flat on his stomach. He swished the bushy limb around in the water, but he saw and felt no sign of the lost corn knife.

"I bet she's sunk way down deep in," he said, "over our heads."

Wilma looked at Dick. "You want to try, Dick?" she asked.

Then she saw that Dick was shaking. It was a hot summer day

and the sun was shining, but Dick was shaking. She felt his hands and they were cold to her touch. The boy's chest looked little and thin with his shirt stuck to it wet and tight. She put her arm around his skinny shoulders.

"I've got to get you home quick," she said. "We'll forget the corn knife. Come on, Margy."

Without a word to Elmer Ruden, the three children went back across the pasture. Elmer watched them go. Then he loped across the field, found his bicycle and rode off down the road whistling.

Back at the barnyard Wilma said, "We might as well tell Dad and get it over with, Dick. Don't you think so?"

"Yes," said Dick. "It was an old corn knife anyway, but still . . . I suppose he didn't want me to lose it."

Dad was by the barn grinding ear corn. The children came up and Wilma shouted, "Dick lost the corn knife, Dad." She had to shout very loud so he could hear above the clatter of the noisy machine. Dad had the scoop shovel in his hands. He came over to hear better.

"I . . . I dropped the corn knife in the creek!" yelled Dick.

"IN THE CREEK?" shouted Dad. "What were you doing with the corn knife in the creek?"

Angry and annoyed, Dad started toward the boy, scoop shovel in hand. Then he saw him—wet, dripping and covered with mud. He stopped in his tracks. One look was enough.

"Dog-gone-it!" he cried. "What next. Won't that kid ever get any sense?" To Wilma he said, "Take him in the house and tell Mom to put him to bed."

CHAPTER VII

In the Cornfield

"Why doesn't she come?" asked Margy.

"She'll come as soon as they bring her," said her mother.

Supper was over and all the chores were done. The family sat around and waited. They were all eager for Wilma to get back from her first job—detasseling corn. Dad had driven her to town that morning at six-thirty. From there, with a group of farm and town girls, she was driven in a truck to the Seed Company's farm. Every six female rows of the hybrid seed corn had to have the tassels removed, leaving two male rows with tassels for spreading the pollen. This was done so that the ears produced on the female cornstalks would be pure seed.

It was growing dark when a car stopped at the end of the lane—the Hasses' car. The tall, slim figure of a growing girl came running in. Wilma wore a wide-brimmed straw hat, old blouse and jeans, ankle socks and her oldest shoes. She was red-faced and hot, covered with dirt and dust. When she got to the porch, she staggered and slumped down on the couch.

"Jeepers!" she cried out. "It's good to be back. I'm ready for a bath. I feel like I've been eating dirt."

"The water is heating in the wash-house," said Mom.

Everybody began to talk at once.

"How did you like it?" asked Dick.

"Was the work hard?" asked Mom. "Could you reach the tassels?"

"Aw—look at that sunburn!" said Raymond. "Your neck is burnt to a crisp. You've spoiled your good looks forever."

"How hot was it—one hundred and twenty degrees out in the sun at noon?" asked Dad.

Wilma caught her breath and began to answer. "It was chilly on the ride over. We started out in slacks and sweaters. By noon we were down to shorts and halters."

"Did you bring some of your lunch back to me?" asked ever-hungry Margy.

"No," said Wilma. "I ate every bit of it—all four of those meat sandwiches, the fruit and cookies and potato chips and the candy bar. Then I wished I'd left the potato chips and candy bar at home. They made me too thirsty. And what do you think? They won't give you enough water."

"They won't?" asked Mom. "Why not?"

[95]

Wilma pulled out her collapsible drinking cup to show them.

"I carry this in my pocket, and if I lose it, I pay twenty-five cents. Our crew foreman, Ernie Welker, told us not to drink too much water or it would make us sick. They have water in milk cans at the ends of the row, but the rows are about a mile long."

"What's this you're wearing?" asked Margy.

"That's my badge," said Wilma. "It says *Standard Seed Company* and it's got my number on it. If I lose my badge, I pay twenty-five cents to replace it."

"But what did you *do* all day?" asked Dick.

"DO?" cried Wilma. "I pulled tassels ALL DAY LONG for six solid hours! Tassels, tassels, tassels! I'm sick of them. We go over the rows not once, but three times. The first time we take all the tassels we can see. The second time, we feel for them and take everything. The third time we take suckers and all the tassels lower down."

Dick said, "I don't see anything hard about that."

"You don't, eh?" said Wilma. "Well, I do. At the end of the first hour I thought I was going to die. After the first row I was going to quit. I got me a drink. I took the second row and it made me feel discouraged. Then I just put away the thought and kept on. I tried to think about what I'll do with my money."

"Why did you get so discouraged?" asked Dick.

"It's hard work, that's why," said Wilma. "You walk and stretch and reach as high as you can reach. Most of that corn is ten feet high already. I never saw such corn before. I'd like to meet the guy that invented it and tell him what I think of him! The pollen fell down on my neck and arms and stung me. My arm and shoulder just ached. I felt sorry for the short girls. You can't sit down and rest every two feet. You have to keep on going. If you get behind, they'll fire you. Some of the girls got sick."

"What did they do?" asked Mom.

"They went to the truck to lie down," said Wilma. "The truck is parked out on the road in the hot sun. You can lie *under* it, but that's no fun either."

"Did Rita and Donna go, too?" asked Raymond.

"Sure," said Wilma, "and we had the most fun . . ."

"Fun?" cried Raymond. "I thought this was hard work."

"We had fun, too," said Wilma. "We laughed and sang and kidded each other all the way over in the truck and all the way back. It took us two hours to get to the field. Gosh! That truck seat was so hard and the road so bumpy. We had to sit on planks—thirty-nine of us, three crews. There's a canvas over the top to keep the dust off."

"Two hours each way?" asked Dad. "Where did they take you?"

"Heavens, I don't know," said Wilma. "Way off in the central part of the state somewhere. The roads were all new to me. We get paid for one way in the truck, so we don't mind how far we go."

Wilma stopped talking at last to have her bath and eat supper.

The next night when she returned, Wilma felt better.

"I'm getting stronger every day," she cried, showing her arm muscle.

"And your nose is getting redder," said Dick.

"But a lot of girls got sick today," she went on. "Nobody wanted any lunch. Those who tried to eat brought up their din-

[97]

ners. Ernie gave them a bawling out and said they drank too much water. But gee! It sure was hot. When Ernie saw some lying inside the truck and others on the ground underneath, he took one look and said, 'I've seen battlefields that looked better than this!' He made all the kids laugh."

"I bet they were just playing sick," said Dick.

"No, they weren't," said Wilma. "We don't get paid for the time we're sick, so that don't get you anywhere. We get sixty cents an hour on weekdays and a dollar an hour on Sundays. And if we work through to the end, we'll get an extra bonus of fifteen cents per hour for the whole time."

"Why do you work Sundays?" asked Dad.

"That's what we asked Ernie," said Wilma. "He said the corn grows on Sundays just the same as on weekdays. But the tassel season will be over in three weeks, thank goodness. By August, I'll be ready for vacation."

"Vacation? Where are we going?" asked Dick.

Everybody looked at Dad. "We'll take our vacation at home this year. Unless somebody wants to go in town and visit Uncle Henry."

The children groaned and Mom and Dad laughed.

On Saturday, at the end of her first week, Wilma came home jubilant. She had her first pay check in hand. She waved it in all their faces. Supper was over and everybody was dressed up, ready to go to town.

"Going to spend it in town tonight?" asked Dad.

At first Wilma was eager to go. But by the time she got a meal ready for herself, and had her bath, she was too tired. She climbed the stairs wearily, threw off her clothes and dropped into bed. Before she knew it, she was sound asleep.

One morning during Wilma's second week, Dad drove her to town at the usual time. After he returned, he and Raymond went to the Heiters' to help shell corn. Mom and Dick and Margy were left at home alone. After Dick's ducking in the creek, he had spent several days in bed and been told to get plenty of rest. He was just beginning to be active again. He didn't mind his crutches any more.

Mom went to the garden to gather cucumbers. "I'm going to make pickles," she said.

About ten o'clock, Mrs. Hass drove in. She had her three small children with her—Susan and Peggy and Robert. Mom and Mrs. Hass began to compare pickle recipes. Dick went out to the hen-house and the children followed. The door had been closed all night to keep varmints away. When Dick opened it, a large fat goose came waddling out. It stumbled over the board across the sill and came down on its stomach *kerplunk!*

"That's Mother Goosey," said Dick. "She never will learn anything. She stumbles over that board every morning."

The children laughed. A large white rooster with a red head and long tail feathers jumped out. Other geese and hens followed.

"That's Peaches!" said Dick, pointing to the rooster.

"How did he get that name?" asked Robert.

"When he was little, he always kept saying *purch, purch, purch,*" said Dick, "so I named him Peaches."

Peaches started to peck Mother Goosey to make her go back in.

"Watch!" said Dick. "Mother Goosey don't like Peaches."

Another goose got behind Peaches and started pulling his tail

[99]

feathers out. All the geese began to peck him. By this time
Peaches had had enough. He ran back in the corner of the henhouse and hid himself.

"They fight him every morning," said Margy. "Poor Peaches!"

Now the geese were stretching. Across the barnyard they went,
flapping their wings and honking loudly.

"See?" laughed Dick. "Mother Goosey is still boss of the
barnyard!"

The children liked Dick and his stories. "Tell us some more,"
they begged.

"Tell them how the hens talk, Dick," said Margy.

Dick sat down in the henhouse doorway. Mother Goosey came
back and he took her on his lap and stroked her neck. The children crouched near by to listen. Dick made the sounds of a hen's
clucking.

"The mother hen says, 'Danger! Hawk's coming!' or maybe
she says, 'Dog or man around.' At night she purrs to put the
chicks to sleep. She keeps saying, 'Go to sleep, go to sleep, don't
wake up till morning.' " He imitated all the sounds with henlike
clucks.

"Tell what she says when a chick gets lost," said Margy.

"The chick says, 'Hey, Mom, I'm lost.' And the mother hen
answers, 'Here I am, here I am, come right over here where
I am.' "

"You sound just like an old hen clucking, Dick," said Robert.

"Sure," said Dick, "I'm first cousin to the hens and the geese.
Now I've got to water the hogs."

The children jumped up and Susan Hass said, "Let's play
hide-and-seek." Margy and the others agreed. They ran over by
the barn and the corncrib where there were plenty of places to

hide. The eighty-acre cornfield was just over the fence behind the hog-house. Robert started the game by being *it*. He began to count to one hundred by fives.

Margy knew all the best hiding places. She tried the corncrib first. She climbed in the crib with the ear corn. She stepped up on the pile and stumbled. The whole mass of piled-up corn above her began to move. It frightened her for a minute. She slipped and lost her footing again. The pile began to tumble. Heavy ears came down and hit her on head and shoulders.

"Wow! Dog-gone-it!" she said, jumping up. "I'm going to get out. They'll see me in here anyhow. They can see right through the cracks."

She climbed out the small window where Dick scooped corn to feed the hogs. Over the fence like a little squirrel she went. Across the hog lot, over another fence and into the cornfield.

"Robert will never find me now," she said.

She ducked in between the rows. The stalks of corn were so huge and the leaves were so large now, it was like a dense forest. Even when the sun was highest at midday, the lower leaves were still damp and cool. It was like being in the shade of a great big tree, of many, many trees. It was much shadier than the grove. It was a good place to cool off. Margy looked back. She was sure no one could see her now.

"Eighty-five, ninety, ninety-five, ONE HUNDRED!"

Margy heard Robert's triumphant shout. She heard the dogs barking. She smiled. Robert had probably caught Susan and Peggy already, and they were all hunting for her, looking everywhere. She was supposed to stay in one place now. She stopped running and caught her breath. She waited.

She waited a while and they did not come. She smiled to her-

[101]

self. They would never find her this time. They would never even think of the cornfield. She remembered the day when Mom and the whole family came out to pull cockleburrs. She remembered how she made up a game of "going through doors." She began to walk again. She went down the shady row until she came to an open place where a hill of corn was missing. She stepped through the door into the next room. She walked down that row. She forgot about hide-and-seek. She played she was in a great big house with many rooms and windows and doors. It was fun going in and out of doors. She kept on walking.

Meanwhile, back at the house, Mrs. Hass was calling, "Robert! Susan! Peggy!"

"What do you want, Mom?" answered Robert.

"It's time to go now," said Mrs. Hass.

The Hass children ran to their mother and they all climbed in their car. Mrs. Hass and Mom talked a while. Then Mrs. Hass turned on the starter.

"Where's Margy, Susan?" asked Mom.

"Oh," laughed Susan, "we never found her. We were playing hide-and-seek. She's still hiding."

Mom looked at Dick. "Did you see her, Dick?"

"No," said Dick. "She's pretty good at finding new places to hide."

The Hasses drove down the lane and out the road. Mom and Dick went back in the house. Dick found a piece of cake to eat. Mom called out the back door, *"Mar-gy! Mar-gy!"*

Buster came running up and Dick fed him. He whistled for Popcorn but the little dog did not come.

"Go look in the barn and the corncrib," said Mom. "See what she is up to. Tell her the Hass children have gone. She can come in now."

Dick looked in all the buildings. He called Margy by name. But he saw nothing of his little sister. Buster sniffed in every corner. She wasn't there. Dick hated to go back in and tell Mom. But it was very strange for Margy to disappear like this.

"She's not out there," Dick announced flatly. "I can't find her."

"Oh, she's hiding somewhere," said Mom cheerfully. "She's trying to play a joke on us. We'll just wait till she decides to come in."

Mom went ahead with her pickles. She measured out the salt to make the brine. She got out her jars and sterilized them. She turned on the radio and listened to her favorite program as she filled the jars.

But Dick was not satisfied. He went the rounds of the buildings again. This time he included the henhouse, the hayloft, the cattle lean-to, the granary and the tool house. They were all empty with a silence that was ominous. Soon Mom came out to join him. She had a worried look on her face.

"I can't see where that child has gone," she said. "She's five—old enough to know better."

Mom went into the cattle lot and looked in the stock tank. Nothing there but a couple of Dick's goldfish swimming around. She looked in the cattle shed, in the stall where the new bull calf was penned. She looked in the pen where Goldie and her calf were lying down. But Margy was not there. Mom's and Dick's shouts echoed back and forth.

"Run, Dick, look through the grove," Mom said. "Maybe she's hiding in some of that broken-down machinery."

Soon Dick came back. "She's not there, Mom."

"Did you look up in the trees, Dick?"

"What would she be doing up in a tree?" laughed Dick.

"She might have found a bird's nest," said Mom. "Or she might just be hiding—to keep us looking for her."

But Margy was not in any of the trees.

"I'm worried," said Mom at last. "You take the tractor, Dick, and drive over to Bill Heiter's and tell Dad we can't find her. Tell him and Raymond to come home right away. I'll call up Loretta Hass and see if the children know anything more."

Mom went to the telephone, cranked the handle and called the number. It was a party line and a busy one. All the neighbor women heard Mrs. Hoffman say that Margy was lost. Mrs. Hass questioned her children. They repeated that Margy ran off to hide and must still be hiding. They did not know where.

Dick should have been glad to drive the new tractor. It was the first time he had been allowed on it since cultivating time in June. But now he hardly thought about it. He started the engine and began to drive automatically. All his former pleasure in the machine was gone. He wished with all his heart he could solve the puzzle of where Margy had gone. She must be just fooling them. But she was so smart, she might keep on fooling them for a long time before she showed up.

Mrs. Hass was the first one to come. She brought her three children and came right back again. She offered to drive to the Heiters' to bring the men, but Dick had already gone. Soon other neighbors began to drop in—the Rudens, the Sanders, the Ludwigs and Shutes. By the time Dick got back with Dad and Raymond and Mr. Heiter, the lane and barnyard were full of neighbors' cars and trucks. It was noon now, time for midday dinner. Some of the women had brought food along. They put it on the table but no one thought of eating.

Mrs. Hass and Mom and Dad and several men talked things over.

"It boils down, then, to the creek, the weeds by the road and the cornfield," Mark Hoffman told the men.

The men divided into teams and spread out over the farm. Half of them entered the cornfield—the big eighty. Dick started in with them, but Mom called him back.

"One lost child is enough," said Mom. "I don't want two."

"But, Mom, I'm eleven—not five," protested Dick. "I can find my way. Last year I drug and disced this whole eighty. This year I cultivated it. I know all the twists and turns in the corn rows.

I know right where they come out on the other side."

But Mom would not listen. She had been crying, but now had dried her tears. There was a fierce look in her face, a look that showed she would never give up. Everywhere she went, she kept calling aloud in a voice of pain: *"Mar-gy! Where are you, Mar-gy?"* Those who heard her cry of anguish knew they would never forget it.

Mrs. Hass took Mom back in the house to try to comfort her. Mrs. Ruden and the other women searched the ditches and uncut weeds by the road. Mom phoned Aunt Etta in town. Uncle Henry hurried out after he finished his day's work. He brought Aunt Etta and three men from the factory with him. He sent the men down to the creek to drag the water hole.

Dick watched them. He could have told them it was a waste of time. He had seen no footprints along the creek. He knew Margy had not been there. The only thing the men found was the lost corn knife. Dick took it back to the tool house. It was rusted and would need sharpening. He wondered if Dad would be glad to get it back.

When Dick came out of the tool house, he saw Buster and called him over. Then he whistled for Popcorn, but Popcorn did not come. He had a special whistle just for Popcorn. Popcorn always recognized it and came. Dick sat down and patted Buster.

"Where did Popcorn go?" he asked.

Buster stretched out and panted. He had been running back and forth, excited over all the visitors. Now he was tired.

Dick began to think. When did he last see Popcorn? He remembered. It was in the morning, after the Hasses came. The little kids began to play hide-and-seek. Popcorn had chased little

Peggy and scared her. Margy had said, "Oh, Pie Face won't hurt you, Peggy. He's our pet. He sleeps in my bed at night." Then Popcorn had run along with them.

Dick jumped up suddenly.

"I bet he's with her right now," said Dick. "If I can find Popcorn's tracks, they'll lead me to the place where she is hiding. If I can find Popcorn, he'll follow her."

Dick ran over to the barn where the game of hide-and-seek had started. In a short time, he entered the cornfield behind the hog lot. He whistled now and then as he walked along, his eyes on the ground. Maybe Margy had fallen asleep somewhere. Dick had once found her asleep on top of a strawstack out in the field. She must be asleep. That was why she did not answer.

It was beginning to grow dark when Dick came out on the other side of the big eighty. Now a little rat terrier dog scampered

beside him. He came out on the highway and looked in both directions, uncertain which way to go. A large truck thundered past but did not stop.

Dick's legs were aching. He wished he had brought his crutches. He wondered how many miles he had walked in the cornfield. A half-hour before when Popcorn heard Dick's whistle and came bounding up to greet him, Dick thought his search was over. But the dog did not lead him to Margy. The dog kept running in circles and Dick became more and more confused. He decided to get out to the road somewhere—anywhere, to get his bearings. On the road, Popcorn did not help him either. Dick could not decide whether to go to the right or the left. He had the feeling that Margy had come out to the road. She might have been picked up by a car. It had all been a wild-goose chase. He might as well go home. He'd better get home before Mom found out he had gone through the cornfield. That would only make her worry more. He decided to ask for a ride from the next car or truck that came along.

He heard the truck long before it got there. He heard the singing voices of the girls, so he knew it was the detasselers coming home. Wilma would be on the truck. Russell Ruden would be driving. Russell would stop and give him a ride.

The girls' young voices rang out clearly:

"O, come all detasselers
And listen to me,
Never stake out your fortune
On a detasseler's fee.
The leaves they will wither,

The roots they will die;
You'll be without money
And never know why!"

Dick picked Popcorn up in one arm and waved with the other. Russell Ruden, Elmer's older brother, pulled up to a sudden stop. The girls in the body of the truck shrieked.

"What's the matter, Russ?" "Run over somebody, Russ?" "Oh, hurry up, Russ, I'm hungry, I want to get home," called the girls.

Some one began to sing:

"Merrily we bump along, bump along,
Merrily we bump along, o'er the dusty roads!"

A car came up from the other way and stopped beside the crew truck. A detasseler shouted to the driver, "Don't you see us? Can't you hear us?"

"I heard you all right," answered the driver. Dick saw that it was Bill Heiter. "A load of hogs went through just before you girls came along. You girls made just a little more noise than the hogs!"

The detasselers roared with laughter.

"Say, Russ," said Bill Heiter. "You didn't pass a little girl walking along the road anywhere, as you came along. Did you?"

"What do you mean?" asked Russell Ruden.

"The Hoffman girl is lost . . . been gone since early morning," said Bill Heiter. "Eight hours already and night's coming."

"Oh yes, we saw her," said Russell. He began to grin.

Dick still standing in the road, tense with fear, could not move.

[109]

He wondered what Russell found funny about it. He clasped Popcorn tighter. The touch of the dog was a comfort to him.

"Where was she?" asked Bill. "We're cruising around on all the roads in the county now. We think she's been picked up by a car . . . or kidnapped maybe . . . Where was she?"

"Oh, back a ways," said Russ Ruden, still grinning. He pointed back with his thumb. Russ had the reputation of being a great tease.

"About how far?" cried Bill Heiter. "She had on a blue dress and her feet were bare, and her hair is brown, in two short pigtails. Did she look like that? Are you sure? Where was she?"

Russell Ruden reached over and started his engine.

"Get in, Dick," he said. "Crowd in here between me and Ernie." Dick found he was able to move. He climbed in. "She's back in there with her big sister, Bill," Russ went on. "Now, that's a good joke on you!"

"Where? In your truck? You mean you've found her?" yelled Bill Heiter.

"Sure," said Russ. "She was walking along the road. Her sister Wilma spotted her and made me drive back half a mile to pick her up. Her sister gave me heck for driving by so fast. Made me back up all that distance. If Wilma wasn't so pretty . . ."

"Well, why on earth didn't you *tell* me?" shouted Bill.

"Heck!" said Russell Ruden. "How was I to know the kid was lost? All she said was she wanted a ride with the detasselers. Said she wanted to sing with 'em too."

"Well!!!" said Bill Heiter. "With all the county out looking for her—I bet there's fifty men . . ."

"You don't say," grinned Russ. He looked at Dick and Ernie

[110]

Welker. "Say! I'll be a hero, won't I? Bringin' her home! Any reward out?"

Bill Heiter and Dick looked inside the truck. There they saw Margy sitting safely in her big sister's arms. They breathed a prayer of gratitude. Then Bill spoke to Russ again.

"I'll turn around and drive on ahead and tell the folks the good news. Honk your horn as loud as you can. That's the signal if she's found. We'll both honk all the way to Hoffman's."

When the honking car and truck reached the barnyard, everybody had guessed the good news. People came running in from all directions. Margy jumped down off the rear end of the truck straight into her mother's arms. Mom held her for a long time and did not want to let her go.

Then Margy said, "I can hide so no one can find me, can't I?"

Mom did not know whether to praise her or scold her. She managed to say, "Don't ever do it again, Margy. Don't ever go in the cornfield."

"I liked it at first," said Margy, "but after a while, I couldn't find my way out. So I just lay down with Sassy Brat and took a nap."

The listening people laughed now with relief.

Wilma looked around, bewildered. She, Wilma, was not the center of attention tonight. Nobody looked at her or at the other detasselers, tired and weary, in the truck. This was one night when the tale of their day's adventures had to wait. There was only one story and it was on everybody's lips, "The little Hoffman girl has been found unharmed."

Dick took Margy by the hand and led her to the house.

"I knew we'd find her, Mom," he said.

CHAPTER VIII

The White Pigeon and the Sick Hog

For the next two days after Margy was found, Dick had to stay in bed. His long trudge through the cornfield had tired him and made his rheumatism worse. On the third day, he felt rested again, so Dad dropped him off at the Rudens' on his way to town. Dick had not seen Elmer lately.

Elmer and his sister, Donna, had a stepladder at the back of their house.

"Hello, what you doing?" asked Dick.

"Tearing down sparrows' nests," said Elmer.

Donna said, "Sparrows are no good. They just mess up the place."

"The Vet told us to clear them all out of our hog-house," said Dick. "They carry cholera germs."

"They're building nests under the eaves up here," said Donna. "They make so much noise, they wake us up every morning." She ran indoors and came out with a handful of red ribbons, cut in short lengths. "Mom said to tack red ribbons up. The birds are afraid of something that dangles and blows in the wind. The ribbons will keep them from building again."

Two large sparrow nests were under the eaves at the back door. They were big and messy, full of white chicken feathers. The sparrows were building a third nest around the corner. As the children came up, they flew off to a tree, chirping noisily.

Elmer climbed up the ladder and pulled the nests down. He threw them on the ground. Dick climbed up after him and tacked the red ribbons in place, while Donna watched from below.

"After dark," said Elmer, "you can go out to that tree and catch a sparrow in your hand."

"You can?" said Dick.

"Oh yes," said Elmer. "They can't see too good. Last night I caught about twenty of them."

"What did you do with them?" asked Dick.

"Fed them to our dog Pooch," said Elmer. "He likes them. All but three. I gave them to the cat."

"Do you just pick them off the limb of a tree?" asked Dick.

"Yes," said Elmer. "They roost there after dark."

"They don't hear us coming," said Donna. "We go kinda tip-toeing."

"Oh!" said Dick. "I should think destroying their nests would be enough. That ought to make them go somewhere else."

[113]

"Not with sparrows," said Elmer. "They come right back and build another nest. My Dad says they're the worst pests on the place—except pigeons."

"You don't like pigeons?" asked Dick.

"They're terrible," said Elmer. "They follow the cows around and scare them. They even ride on their backs!"

"They like the loose corn," said Dick. "That's why they are always around a corncrib. Ours never get tame. They land on a shed and just talk to us. You walk up to them and they fly away."

"Some people like to eat them," said Donna.

"*We* do," said Elmer. "I'll get my BB gun and we'll shoot some and ask Mom to cook them for dinner."

"We used to have a pure white pigeon that stayed on our barn," said Donna.

"A pure white one would be pretty," said Dick.

Elmer brought out his BB gun and the children went to the barnyard. A row of pigeons sat on the roof of the barn.

"They make good targets," Elmer said, "sitting on the roof like that. It's so easy to shoot up."

Mr. Ruden came out and said, "Hi, Dick." He brought his shotgun. He turned to Elmer and said, "You let Dick shoot first. Give him your BB gun."

"No," said Dick. "I don't want to shoot."

"It's safe," said Mr. Ruden. "When you aim up, you're not likely to hit someone. I always tell the kids to shoot *up*."

"It's not that," said Dick. "I know it's safe. I'm not afraid of hitting people. I just don't want to hit pigeons."

"You don't?" Elmer and his Dad laughed. Elmer explained, "Dick likes to make pets out of pigeons too, I suppose."

"What would I want to kill one for?" asked Dick. "I figure a pigeon likes to be alive just as much as a person does. Why kill it?"

Elmer and Mr. Ruden said nothing, but Donna spoke up, "Dick thinks they're cute and so do I."

"They're good to eat," said Elmer.

"It's a lot of work to pick the feathers and dress the little things," said Donna. "Mom hates it. It takes about four for a meal for a family like ours. Mom roasts them in the oven."

"They're good for fish bait, too," said Mr. Ruden.

"Oh boy," said Elmer, "do the fish ever go for pigeon bait! Pop, if we get one, let's you and me go fishing."

Mr. Ruden smiled and cocked his gun. After the first shot, the pigeons on the roof flew away. Pooch, the dog, jumped around, excited.

"There's hundreds more roosting up in the hayloft," said Elmer.

"I'll tell you what I'll do," said Dick. "I'll go up in the hayloft and chase more pigeons out for you."

Dick was glad to get away from the shooting. He climbed the ladder into the hayloft and after each shot, he chased a few pigeons out of the top window. He counted six shots of the shotgun and two of the BB gun. Then he heard the dog barking and general excitement. Maybe they had killed one.

But Dick was not listening any more. He did not care what the Rudens were doing. He had found a young pigeon—a pure white one. It was sitting on a joist above the hay. It could fly only a little way. He picked it up and it showed no fear. He stroked its neck. He cuddled it in his hands.

"You're not hurt, are you, Susanna?"

He had a name for it already. He would feed it and tame it. Soon it would eat out of his hand. It was so young, it would make a nice pet.

When Dick came down, the Rudens were excited over the pigeon Elmer had shot. Pooch had brought it back and Mr. Ruden was cutting it up for fish bait. They were starting off for the creek to go fishing.

Only Donna looked at the white pigeon.

"It's cute," she said, "with its pink eyes. That white one I used to see must have been this one's mother."

"Do you want it?" Dick held the pigeon out to her. "Take it. It's yours. It will make a nice pet."

"Oh, you take it, Dick," said Donna. "We don't fool with pets around here the way you do. I'm going fishing with Elmer and Dad. Don't you wan't to go, too?"

"No," said Dick. "I'm going home. So long."

He watched Donna go running across the barnyard to join her father and brother. He himself took off in the opposite direction, across the fields toward home. He knew just what he would do. He would make a cage out of chicken wire. He would have to keep Susanna in a cage while she was so young. He must keep her safe from the dogs and cats.

Back home, he showed the white pigeon to Margy. He let her hold it a while. He put it down on the ground. It walked a few steps, then he caught it again. He went to the tool house and Margy held the pigeon while he wired a cage together. He brought bread and milk and the pigeon ate. He put Susanna in her cage and hung the cage up on the house porch. He covered it with a cloth and the bird went to sleep, making cooing noises.

Mom made a fuss about the pigeon. She was tired of having pets in the house. She reminded Dick of the runt Squeaky, the sow Susie, the rabbit Peter, the rooster Peaches, the goose Mother Goosey, the chipmunk Chippy, the dog Popcorn, to say nothing of old Buster.

"Haven't you enough pets?" she asked.

"No," said Dick. "I'm trying to find a young woodchuck now. They tame easy, and I'll name him Chucky. I've always wanted a lizard or a salamander. You don't have to feed them—they live off of air! And I'll never be happy until I get a raccoon."

"You can't keep wild things penned up," Mom reminded him. "You always have to let them go again."

"I know it," said Dick. "They come and they go. Susie and Peter and Chippy are gone. Squeaky and Peaches and Mother Goosey are still here. And Popcorn—I don't know what I'd do without Popcorn."

Popcorn began to bark at Susanna, and Dick scolded him.

But as much as he wanted to keep her, the white pigeon did not stay long. The next time Dick took her out, she started to fly. She flew up on the peak of the kitchen roof and sat there. Dick brought a ladder and climbed to the top.

He edged up over the roof as gently as he could. Susanna's bright eye kept watching him. He picked her up and held her. At the edge of the roof stood a tall lightning rod. It had a beautiful blue glass ball for ornament. Dick looked at the colors in the ball—the bird's white feathers and its shining pink eye. He could see all the red farm buildings with their sharp white trim reflected in it. He held the pigeon up beside the blue glass ball and let her study her reflection. Then he climbed down and put her back in her cage.

That same evening, Margy left the door of Susanna's cage open. The pigeon flew out across the porch. Then it fluttered out the door and landed on the ground. Bob-bob, the cat, asleep on the walk, woke up and made a dash for the bird. But Dick got there first and rescued his pet.

He could feel the bird's heart beating when he picked her up.

"That was a close call, Susanna," he said. "You stay in your cage now, like a good girl."

The next day he hung the cage out in the cedar tree in the house yard. After Susanna learned to fly, he left the cage door open every day. He wanted her to feel free and get used to her freedom. She knew her home and came back to it for rest and sleep. She began to fly with the other pigeons in the feed lot,

where they found plenty of grain. Dick did not need to feed her.

After a while she stopped coming. Sometimes Dick would see a white pigeon in the flock at the barn. Sometimes he searched for her in vain. There was no white one to be seen.

"Where have you gone, Susanna?" he cried. "Have you left me for good?"

It was Saturday, the last day of Wilma's detasseling job. She came home at four o'clock, wearing a cotton dress, which she had taken with her that morning. She had her final check to show and exciting news to tell the family.

"We worked only half a day," she said. "There wasn't much to do, the field was so clean. But Flossie Miller stepped on a snake and all the girls ran to the truck! In the afternoon we had a picnic. They took us down by a creek and we all went wading. We ducked each other to get clean—and we ducked Russell and Ernie too. Then the boys sliced watermelons and how we did eat! After that, guess what we did."

"Tell us, tell us," cried Margy.

"We changed to our dresses inside the truck," Wilma went on. "Ernie built up a big bonfire for us. We threw all our dirty blouses and jeans on the fire and watched them burn, while we sang all the songs we knew. We sang till we all got hoarse. De-tasseling was hard work and we were glad it was over—until next year."

"What will you do now?" asked Dick.

"Have a big shopping spree for back-to-school clothes," said Wilma. "Can we go to town, Dad?"

"It's Saturday night," said Dad with a smile. "When would

we ever see our friends if we didn't go to town on Saturday night? Who wants spending money?"

Dad tossed a quarter to Margy and a half dollar to Dick. "How much did you make all together?" he asked Wilma.

"Seventy dollars," said Wilma proudly.

"Whew!" Dick whistled. "All that for clothes?"

"You buying a trousseau?" teased Raymond.

"I'm going to put half of it in the bank," said Wilma, "and use the other half for clothes. Most of the girls are doing that."

Everybody rushed to get the chores done early. After supper, the family dressed up in neat, freshly washed clothes. Mark Hoffman brought the old Hudson around to the house-yard gate and sounded the horn. Raymond came running in from the barn.

"The hogs are out," he said. "We'll have to get them back in before we go."

"Now who left that gate open?" scolded Dad.

"Nobody," said Raymond. "The hogs rooted it open."

The spring pigs, farrowed in March, had grown into fifty-pound shoats and then, after six months, into two hundred-pound hogs. All summer they had been fed a hearty diet of oats and corn, and fattened on clover. They would soon be ready for market. Whenever they got out of their lot, they did plenty of damage. They rooted up the yard, upset everything moveable and tore up flowers and plants.

"We'll have to get the hogs rings out and fill their snouts," said Dad, "to stop this fence lifting."

Dad and the boys chased the hogs.

"Where's Buster?" shouted Dad. "Where's that dog? Always off somewhere else when you need him."

Dick whistled and Buster came bounding up.

"Bring 'em in, Buster," called Dad. "Nip 'em on the leg and put 'em where they belong."

Buster started bravely after the hogs. But when a fat one turned around and looked at him, the dog ran the other way with his tail between his legs.

"That dog's no good," shouted Dad. "He's a coward."

"He just don't like hogs, Dad," said Dick.

"A hog is like a mule for stubbornness," said Dad. "Always wants to go in the wrong direction."

It was Popcorn who helped most. Soon the hogs were back in the hog lot. Dick ran to see that the gate was tightly closed.

Just inside the fence he saw a hog lying down. He went in and looked at it. It did not move. It was Squeaky grown up, Susie's runt that he had cared for and fattened. He had tamed her and sometimes led her around the barnyard on a leash. He had taught her to sit down politely and beg for an ear of corn. But he had made up his mind not to play with her too much, because then he would hate to see her go when the time came.

What was the matter with Squeaky? He spoke to her, but she did not look up. He rubbed her back of the ears, but she did not respond. She was breathing heavily. He knew she was sick.

Honk! Honk! Raymond was sounding the horn impatiently. Dick came out and closed the gate. He braced it so the hogs could not root it open. He ran for the car. Dad and Raymond were in the front seat, and Mom and the girls were in the back.

"Dad," said Dick, "there's a hog sick down there."

"Sick?" said Dad. "They didn't look sick to me, the way they chased around."

"This one is lying down inside the fence," said Dick. "It's Squeaky."

"Oh, that little runt!" laughed Raymond. "Dick just loves to have his pets get sick . . ."

"So he can doctor them," added Margy. "His name is Doctor Dick!"

"Oh, get in, Dick," said Wilma, "let's go."

"Dad, don't you think we'd better do something?" asked Dick.

"Get in," said Dad. "We're going to town now."

"But Dad—" began Dick.

"It's always this way," said Wilma. "Every time we want to go anywhere, something happens to the hogs."

"I'll stay here, Dad," said Dick.

"Get in," said Dad. "She'll be all right by morning. We're all set to go to town now."

Dick climbed in the car. All the way to town, he listened to Wilma talking clothes with Mom in the back seat.

Town was crowded. All the stores were open and the curbs were lined with parked cars. Town and country people were enjoying a social evening, visiting with each other. They walked up and down the sidewalks of the two blocks where the stores were. Some sat on benches, while others leaned against the fenders of parked cars. They went in the stores and came out with big bundles in their arms.

"I'm going with Dad," said Margy.

"I know why," Dick said to Mom. "Dad will buy her more treats. That's what she thinks."

"Well, I don't want her hanging around us," said Wilma. "Let her go."

Wilma and Mom went into the department store.

"You coming, Dick?"

"No," said the boy.

Raymond strolled off to join a group of older boys, so Dick followed behind Dad and Margy. One side of the street was considered the men's side, the other the ladies'. On the men's side there were two feed stores, a hardware store, the postoffice closed now and several cafés. The men had the coffee habit.

"Come on in, let's have a cup of coffee," said Bill Heiter to Mark Hoffman. They started to enter Muff's Café.

"You stay here with me, Margy," called Dick.

Margy did not look back or listen. She went right in with the men.

"You think you're gonna get a hamburger?" grinned Dick.

Margy nodded and smiled. The screen door closed behind her.

Dick strolled along the street. He passed the Good Morning Feed Store. It had a three-foot chick hatching out of its shell for its trademark. He looked at the metal hens' nests and the gaily colored printed sacks filled with chicken feed. He strolled over to the red and white popcorn stand at the corner. He bought a sack of popcorn and walked along munching it. He stopped and sat down on a bench by the gutter. Inside the store window a television set was running. He watched the program. A stagecoach came dashing up pulled by four galloping horses. He saw the bandits jump up from the bushes and start shooting the passengers. He looked at the other people crowded on the bench and leaning on near-by cars. They all seemed to like it. He got up quickly.

"Hey, where are you going?" asked the person next to him.

Dick looked. It was his cousin Earl, Uncle Henry's boy. "Come, stay here," said Earl. "It's just getting exciting."

Dick walked on. He could not get his mind off that sick hog and he wished he had stayed at home. He crossed the street to the other side. He passed hatless fat men in shirt sleeves and suspenders. He saw Rita Hass and Donna Ruden strolling hand-in-hand with two town girls. He passed women with hair tightly kinked by new permanents. He saw Mrs. Heiter by her car with a wet washcloth, washing her little boy's face. He saw Mr. Hass lifting little Peggy up to drink from the water bubbler at the corner.

"Hello, Dick," said Mr. Hass. "Is it hot enough for you?"

"Sure," said Dick.

"This heat and humidity makes me feel like a steam engine," said Mr. Hass.

"I have to hang my tongue out once in a while to get my breath." The man's voice and the joke sounded familiar.

Dick looked around. There was Uncle Henry. He came up with Aunt Etta and Denny and the twins, Betsy and Patsy. They were all dressed in pretty summer clothes with flowered patterns.

"When you coming out to the farm to see us?" Dick asked the girls.

"Never again," said Betsy, "as long as I live."

"Get rid of all those skunks and we'll come," said Patsy.

Dick laughed. "Oh, we just keep them for *special* visitors."

"Have you seen Earl?" asked Aunt Etta.

"Yes," said Dick. "He's looking at television down by the feed store. Uncle Henry, I found one of the hogs acting sick at home just before we left."

"Sick?" asked Uncle Henry. "What was wrong with it?"

They were standing in front of Dirks' Department Store. Mom and Wilma came out with packages in their arms. Uncle Henry began to joke with Wilma about her detasseling job. The sick hog was forgotten. Wilma told her cousins about the lovely new clothes she was buying with her money.

"Aw, nuts!" Dick turned away. "Let's go home."

"Mom!" cried Wilma. "Dick walks down the street once and he's ready for the car. Why, we only just *came*."

"I want to go home," insisted Dick.

"Mom," Wilma complained. "We can't go anywhere but Dick has to fuss about sick hogs or some old sick pet of his."

Nobody paid any attention to Dick. Dad and Margy saw the family party and came across the street. Dick knew now he was in for a prolonged session. He perched himself up on the hood of somebody's car close at hand.

They all looked at Margy. Margy had always been a pretty child and as the baby, had enjoyed being spoiled. Since her adventure of getting lost in the cornfield, she seldom lost an opportunity to become the center of attention. They were all looking at her now.

"First Mr. Heiter bought me popcorn," the little girl said. "Then Charlie Ruden a sandwich and Grandpa Shute some pop and Dad a hamburger . . ."

"Only *one* hamburger?" asked Uncle Henry.

Margy nodded and went on. "I was still hungry, but they didn't offer me anything more. I had to buy my ice-cream cone myself!"

They all laughed.

"You'd never believe it," said Mom, "but she had a good sup-

per too, before she left home."

"She doesn't look exactly starved," said Aunt Etta. "She'll have to start reducing soon!"

"Margy," said Uncle Henry, "do you still play hide-and-seek in the cornfield?"

"No," smiled Margy happily. "I got cured of that!"

They laughed again.

Uncle Henry turned to Dad and said, "Another week of this heat and we won't have to worry about our corn crop." The men began to talk corn.

Aunt Etta turned to Mom. "I wanted Henry to take us to the show tonight but he wouldn't. Said he had to talk to Mark. Those men—they plant the corn and raise it and harvest it every time they get together—in words. That's all they talk about—corn, corn, corn. I should think you'd be sick to death of it."

"I'm used to it," said Mom. "Besides it's our life, so I like it."

The men debated when to sell last year's corn.

"The corncrib is so full," said Mark, "I'll have to shell to make room for the new crop this fall. Then I also need corn to fatten my hogs for market."

"I need the cash from mine," said Uncle Henry. "Your lease says you'll deliver my share. So go ahead and shell any time now and truck mine to the elevator here in town."

"O. K.," said Mark Hoffman. "I'll find out when Jay Hintz can come."

Dick saw a man he knew. He jumped down from his perch and followed him. It was Doc Musfelt, the old Vet. Here was some one who would listen. The old Vet rubbed his chin thoughtfully after he heard Dick's story.

"With hogs," he said, "you can't tell. They're getting so many new diseases these days. Isolate her at once—that's the first thing. If something gets started, it might go through the whole herd."

"Can you come out and see her?" asked Dick.

"I'm helping my son vaccinate hogs for cholera right now," said Doc. "He's got so many places to go. You come over to the office now. I'll give you some medicine for that sick hog."

They walked to the veterinarian's office. Doc prepared the medicine and told Dick when to give it. "If she's not better by tomorrow," he said, "you phone me and I'll come out and see her."

Dick thanked him, took the package and hurried back to Dirks' Store. The two families were still talking. Denny had fallen down and cut his knee and Aunt Etta was fussing over him.

When Uncle Henry saw Dick, he turned to Dad and said, "Dick tells me you've got a sick hog at home, Mark."

Dad tried to grin, but it was easy to see he was annoyed. "The boy thought it *looked* sick," he said.

Raymond had come over. Now he spoke up, "Doctor Dick takes care of all our sick animals."

But Uncle Henry was not joking this time.

"You're not neglecting a sick hog, are you, Mark?"

"No," said Dad, frowning. "I'll look after it. Let's go home."

"Doc Musfelt gave me something to give to Squeaky," said Dick.

Goodbyes were said and the two families parted. Dad did not speak to Dick all the way home. When they got out of the car, he asked, "What did Doc give you?"

Dick handed him the medicine.

They went out to the hog lot together.

CHAPTER IX

Stubby Tail

"**D**ick! *Raymond!*" Dad's booming voice woke the boys up
out of deep sleep. "Time to get up. Chores to do. Corn
shelling today."

It did not take the boys long to get dressed. Already breakfast
was on the table and Mom had started preparing a big dinner
for a group of hungry men. By seven-thirty, there were two trucks
in the barnyard, several cars, tractors and wagons, and Jay Hintz's
corn shelling machine.

Dick called Popcorn. "Come along, Dum Do Do! You and the
cats will have a busy time today."

The men had started to work. Dick saw Bill Heiter and his

[130]

hired man, Ted Sanders, the two truckers Al Kibler and Emil Spies, Ralph Hass and Grandpa Shute. Soon Uncle Henry Shumaker drove in. He was taking a day off from the factory.

After finishing his chores, Dick went over to watch.

The lower boards on the side of the corncrib had been pried off. A metal trough was placed below to catch the ear corn as it fell out. The men scooped the corn down into the trough with their shovels. Revolving chains in the trough carried the corn to the sheller which stood at one end of the building. A truck was backed up under a bent-over spout.

Jay Hintz had the motor going. The machine made a noisy clatter as the ear corn ran through. Shelled corn came pouring out into the truck. Corncobs came out in a pile at the side. They would be used for many purposes—to burn in the kitchen range, with coal for the tank heater, and in the old stove in the wash-house to heat water for laundry and baths. Other cobs would be dumped in the lane to fill up low spots and make for better traction. A fan blew cornhusks out of the sheller and they dropped in a pile. Later they would be put in the lean-to behind the barn for bedding for the cattle.

"Here's a big strong farmer come out to help us," said Uncle Henry. He poked Dick in the ribs. "Go get your shovel, boy."

Dick laughed. He saw the Rudens' car come in, with Russell and Elmer besides their father. They all got out and Elmer came over to see Dick.

"Hi!" said Elmer. "A little excitement today, huh?"

"Yes," said Dick. "The dogs and cats are excited, too. They don't know which way to jump first."

Jay Hintz kept his eyes on the sheller and an oil can in his hand.

If he heard a funny sound, he tinkered with the engine. Dust and dirt flew in all directions. It settled on the men's faces and eyebrows. They scooped busily, trying to keep up with the machine.

All at once a big rat and several mice came tumbling out. Buster turned tail and ran off, frightened. But Popcorn and the barn cats chased them.

"I'll get me a club," said Elmer. He disappeared and came back with a heavy two-by-four. "I'll club them as they come out."

Dick stood back and said nothing.

"We might scare up a coon or a skunk, Elmer," yelled Ted Sanders. "How would it be to run a skunk through the sheller and take his fur off?"

The men laughed.

"When the Bauers shelled up north of us," shouted Charlie Ruden, "that's just what they did. We could smell skunk down to our place for a whole week."

"Up at Reuters," said Grandpa Shute, "they chased a coon out. Those kids of theirs they caught and tamed it."

"Here's the boy can tame the wild things," said Ted Sanders. He pointed to Dick.

"Dig me out a coon, Ted," said Dick, "but don't run it through the sheller. I prefer to have my pets in one piece."

Dick's Dad worked with the men pushing the corn down. Popcorn got in at his feet, rooting for a rat.

"That dog is death on rats," said Ted Sanders.

"I guess all rat terriers are like that," said Dick.

"Take Popcorn away before I step on him," yelled Dad. "If all this corn comes pouring down on his head, there won't be anything left but a grease spot."

Dick grabbed Popcorn up and tried to hold him. But Buster was barking noisily back of the corncrib. Popcorn jumped out of his arms and dashed around the corner. Dick followed. He tipped over an old oil barrel that stood there, expecting to see a rat. Buster and Popcorn were ready to dash under. But they stopped and backed up. Instead of a rat, Dick saw a snake curled up. Buster took one look at the snake and ran in the other direction.

"Oh! So it's you, is it?" asked Dick, surprised.

"What is it?" yelled Ted Sanders, coming round the corner.

"A snake," said Dick.

"A snake?" Elmer Ruden came running.

By the time Elmer got there, the snake had slid back under the crib. Popcorn began to sniff again. The snake's head appeared. Popcorn barked loudly.

"Let's pull him out," said Ted.

Ted grabbed the snake by the neck and gave a pull. The snake slid back and left him empty-handed.

Elmer turned to Dick. "I bet you're afraid to pick it up."

They waited until the snake's head appeared.

"There! Grab it," said Elmer, "unless you're a sissy."

Dick moved slowly. He picked the snake up carefully. He drew the long body slowly out from its hiding place. He carried it into the empty corncrib and laid it gently on the floor. Popcorn came in and began to bark. The snake started hissing. It struck once or twice but missed the dog.

"I'll get my shovel," said Ted. "I'll kill it for you."

"I'll get my club and help," said Elmer.

Quickly Dick grabbed Popcorn up in his arms. "You mustn't get snakebit, you Twerp." The snake began to move. "Hurry now, quick," said Dick to the snake. "This is your only chance to get away." The snake slid down a hole out of sight.

"Where's the snake?" asked Ted, returning.

"Oh, it got away," said Dick. "It was a harmless bull snake. It will do away with a lot of mice and rats."

"Where's the snake?" asked Elmer, coming back club in hand.

"It got away," said Dick.

"Say, boys," said Ted. "Want me to show you how to make a cornstalk fiddle?"

"Sure," said the boys.

But Mr. Heiter called Ted and he had to go back to work.

"Wait till corn picking time," he said. "Stalks are too green now. You can play a tune on it, too." He went around the barn.

The boys liked Ted, for he was full of ideas.

Dick turned to Elmer. "Did you ever eat a grasshopper?" he asked.

"No," said Elmer. "Whoever thought of such a thing?"

[134]

"Well, Ted told me once if I'd eat a grasshopper, he'd eat one too."

"And did you?" asked Elmer, laughing. "I bet a dollar you did, stupid."

Dick would not say yes or no. Elmer kept pressing him. At last he admitted, "Oh, it was Ted who backed out on it . . ."

Suddenly a terrific clatter was heard. The two boys ran back to the sheller. Jay Hintz whirled around, thinking something had gone wrong with the motor. He stopped the engine quickly and stared in surprise. There was Dick's mother. She had brought a metal bushel basket and was holding it under the spout to fill it with corncobs. They made a loud clatter as they hit the metal of the basket.

"I need a few cobs for the kitchen stove," Mrs. Hoffman explained.

The men laughed.

"Help yourself," said Jay. Then he added, "Just like a woman to scare us to death. I thought my sheller was exploding like an A-bomb! Now, why couldn't she take them off the cob pile?"

"Dick," called Mom, halfway back to the house. "Come and help me."

"I wonder when we get something to eat," said Ted Sanders. He looked toward the back door.

"Here comes lunch," said Grandpa Shute.

Dick and his mother and Wilma brought out a midmorning lunch. Jay Hintz stopped the sheller and Dick passed meat sandwiches and doughnuts around. Wilma poured hot coffee in paper cups. After a short pause for eating, the motor was started again and the men resumed work. As the trucks became filled with the shelled corn, the truckers drove them off to town.

At noon, the men stopped for dinner and a good rest. Up back of the house, they took turns washing hands and faces in two enamel basins on the bench. They pumped cold water from the cistern pump. They slicked up their hair before a small wall mirror on the porch, using comb and brush in an oilcloth pocket there.

Dick came up while the men were washing. Ted Sanders had his hair all slicked up nicely, when suddenly a shower of cold water poured over him. The water bucket and dipper fell to the ground with a clatter. Ted mopped his face with the towel and looked around to see who had thrown it. Dick stepped behind Grandpa Shute. The men all looked innocent. Then they broke into a roar of noisy laughter.

"That's one on you, Ted," said Bill Heiter.

"I was just needin' a cold shower to cool me off," drawled Ted.

"Guess who did it, Ted," piped up Elmer Ruden.

"Never mind, his time's comin'," said Ted.

Dick washed up and went in with the men to the long table.

"Oh, look at our big farmer here!" cried Uncle Henry. "When are you going to do a little farm work and earn your salt, Dick? Are you sure you scooped enough corn to deserve a fine dinner like this?"

"I didn't scoop any," said Dick. "I just—"

All the men were looking at him. His face turned red.

"Sit down, Dick," said Dad quietly. "There's a place beside Elmer."

Dick sat down and Uncle Henry took the place next to Dick. The men began to talk. Mrs. Hoffman had plenty to eat—a large platterful of pork chops, several bowls of mashed potatoes and gravy, coleslaw and mixed salad, pickles and fresh fruit, fruit gelatin and freshly baked rolls and butter. Mom waited on table, keeping the dishes circulating and the men's plates filled. Wilma poured iced tea into their tall glasses.

Dick was hungry and ate fast. He was thirsty too and reached for his glass. He took a big swallow—then looked at the contents of the glass. It was not brown like tea. It was some thick white stuff, but it wasn't milk. He tried to spit it out, but his mouth was filled with bubbles. The more he tried to get rid of them, the more bubbles he made. What did it taste like? Soap! That was it— SOAP!

"What the heck!" mumbled Dick.

"Oh, you took the wrong glass," said Elmer. "That was intended for—"

With one look at Ted, Dick jumped up from the table and ran outside. He had to rinse his mouth many times before he got rid of the taste of soap flakes. Loud guffaws came from the dining room. Dick did not go back to the table again. He knew the men would razz him if he did. Mom brought his plate to the kitchen and he finished eating there.

"I never did a thing to Ted, Mom," said Dick. "I never threw that water on him, but I saw who did it."

"Oh, Ted knows your Uncle Henry did it," said Mom. "Don't worry, he'll take care of *him* all right. Too bad you got hold of Uncle Henry's glass by mistake." Then she added, "They like their little jokes."

After dinner the men went out to work again. The time for joking was over and they were serious again. The shovels scooped the ear corn into the noisy machine as before. Ted Sanders kept promising Dick a raccoon, but none turned up. Buster and Popcorn got tired and ran off to rest in the shade. Dick wandered away. The excitement had all worn off. He was tired but did not like to admit it. He strolled over and looked at the hogs. He spotted Squeaky in the bunch. She was well again now and as fat and frisky as the others. That medicine from Doc Musfelt had saved her in the nick of time.

In the barnyard Russell Ruden sat on Uncle Henry's tractor with a flare box wagon behind. He was starting off to town with a load of shelled corn. Uncle Henry stood talking to him. As Dick passed by, Uncle Henry called him over.

"Bet you'd like to be sitting up there on my tractor and driving to town like Russ, wouldn't you, Dick?" asked Uncle Henry.

"I sure would," said Dick.

"I'll stay here and scoop corn and let you take it in, Dick," said Russ.

"Dad won't let me drive," said Dick, turning away.

Russell started his motor and drove off.

Uncle Henry looked at Dick and said, "Don't you like that nice little tractor of mine any more, Dick?"

"Sure I do," said Dick. "I've never seen a better one."

"When are you going to start being a farmer, Dick?" asked Uncle Henry. "I'm serious about this. At your age, your brother Raymond was driving farm machinery just like a man. Aren't you tired of just standing around all summer and doing nothing? Do you like being a sissy? I should think you'd want to be your Dad's right-hand man."

Dick winced. "I'd sure like to, Uncle Henry—" the boy began.

Dad called just then and Uncle Henry went over to see what was wanted.

Dick stood still, thinking. He wondered if Uncle Henry was right. Maybe he wasn't trying hard enough. Maybe it was all Mom's fault—telling him not to do this and not to do that and keeping him a baby. Maybe if he tried harder, his muscles would get stronger. Maybe he could forget that old rheumatism and do all the things that other boys of his age could do. Some day he would just like to show everybody he was no sissy.

In midafternoon, Dick came bursting into the house.

"Mom!" he called. "Uncle Henry says I can drive his new tractor to town. I'm to take a wagonload of corn in."

"No!" said Mom. "Is Uncle Henry crazy?"

"Dad said I could," insisted Dick. "The truckers went home early and there's only one wagonload still to go. Dad and Uncle Henry both said I could take it." He turned to Margy. "Keep Popcorn in the house, will you? I don't want him to follow me."

Mom said nothing. Margy ran to bring the little dog inside. Mom went to the door and watched. She held her apron to her lips, as she watched the boy drive out the lane. Then she turned back to her work with a worried look on her face.

Dick looked back at the house once. He saw Popcorn looking out of the window of the front room. He smiled to himself, "That little Stubby Tail!" he said. "He wants to go along with me." Dick knew the dog had climbed on the chair and jumped up on the table by the window to look out. "You little old Pie Face! You little old Dumb Do Do—I wish I could take you along with me, but I can't. Goodbye, little Fella, I'll be back soon. You just be a good Stubby Tail and wait for me."

It was good to be driving a tractor again. The sun was hot and bright and Dick could feel it through his cotton shirt. He liked the vibration of the machine. He liked his high perch up on the seat. He had forgotten how wonderful it was. He felt like a king coming down the highway. Wild doves and other birds on the fences and telephone wires scattered and flew away as he came by. He saw several young rabbits scamper off into the bushes.

But he knew he must keep his eyes on the road. He had perfect control of the tractor and was determined not to start dreaming. The road was plenty wide enough for passing other cars, so he was not afraid at all.

"A guy's just got to watch out," he said to himself sternly. "It's only when you are careless that accidents happen."

The elevator stood at the end of Main Street, so Dick did not have to drive where all the cars were. Unloading did not take long, so he was soon on his way home again. It was easier than Dick had thought it would be. The setting sun threw its slanting light across the rolling landscape, lighting the patchwork fields of green and gold with brilliance. The cornstalks, tall and stately now, were bending under the burden of a heavy crop. Dick was conscious only of a wonderful sense of well-being.

His legs did not ache at all. The hot dry sun of summer was helping him. He was better—he would soon be well again. Then he could do all the things that Raymond did so easily. He could prove to Uncle Henry and Elmer Ruden that he was no sissy. He could grow up to be a farmer the way Uncle Henry wanted him to. He could drive a tractor as well as Raymond, as well as Elmer could. He knew as much about a tractor as anybody. He would never tip one over again.

Looking ahead, he saw what looked to be a white newspaper lying in the road.

"Somebody must have dropped one," he thought. "That's funny. Who would drop a newspaper in the road?"

When he came closer, near the bridge over the creek, he pulled up. He stopped the tractor and got off. He walked ahead to look. Then he saw that it was not a newspaper at all.

It was a little white dog lying there, with brown spots on its head. It was Popcorn, a beloved dog with dozens of nicknames—Shicklegruber, Twerp, Hot Dog, Dumb Do Do, Stubby Tail. He looked at his pet for a long time, but he could not go near him. Tears came to his eyes, but he brushed them away, saying aloud, "That's for babies!"

He stood still, trying to sense what had happened. "Somebody

ran over him, with a car or a truck," he said. Was it one of the truckers? No, they had gone home before he started out. It was some car going by.

"They could have missed him!" he cried out in anguish. *"They just wanted to hit him!"*

Then suddenly, Dad was standing there beside him. He had walked past the white object in the road.

"I thought you must be in trouble," said Dad. "I saw the tractor stopped out here. Did you get along all right?"

Dick sniffed once or twice. "Oh, sure," he said.

"What's the matter, boy?" asked Dad.

"Look there." Dick pointed.

"I saw it," said Dad. "Too bad." Mark Hoffman picked the dog's limp body up and laid it in the ditch. "I'll come back for him later. Hop on, I'll drive you back to the house."

Dick hopped on the tractor and caught hold of the fender.

"We'll have to think of the others," Dad said. "Don't break the news too quickly. They're fond of the dog too." He started the motor.

Mom was waiting at the door. When she saw Dick's face, her heart fell. "Oh, I just knew something would happen," she began. "Did you have an accident? Are you hurt? What's the matter?"

"I'm all right," said Dick in a lifeless voice.

Mom turned to Dad. "What's he crying about?"

Dick turned angrily. "I'm not crying!" he said.

Wilma and Raymond and Margy all stood listening. Dad tried to tell them gently. Finally he had to come right out with the truth. "Oh, Popcorn's got run over," he said.

[142]

The news stunned them all. Mom spoke first.

"Margy," she said, "before Dick left, didn't you bring Popcorn in the house like he told you to?"

"Yes," said Margy. "Popcorn jumped up on the table and watched Dick go. Then he ran to the door and whined, so I let him out."

There was no use scolding Margy now. It was too late.

"He must have followed you, Dick," said Mom sadly. "He always liked to be with you."

"I'll go out and bury him," said Dad. "Want to come along, Dick?"

"No," said Dick. *"And don't tell me where."*

Wilma ran upstairs crying. Raymond began to talk about the rats and mice Popcorn had caught at the corncrib.

Uncle Henry breezed in just before he left to go to town. Dick was lying on the couch on the porch.

"Well!" said Uncle Henry. "I'm proud of you, Dick! It takes your old Uncle Henry to manage things. If I were around here all the time, I'd make a man of you yet. You could be driving that tractor all the time and be a big help to your Dad."

"He's not old enough to be a hired man, Henry Shumaker!" said Mom with spirit. "And when he is, you'll pay him for his work."

"Why, Bertha, he drove that tractor to town as well as any man could do it," said Uncle Henry. "Brought it home without a scratch on it."

"What did you expect him to do, bring it home in pieces?"

"Now, Bertha," began Uncle Henry. "I'm only saying I'm proud of the boy. What's wrong with that?"

Dad came back in. He had heard Uncle Henry's loud voice. He took Uncle Henry in the front room and told him what had happened.

Uncle Henry came back, filled with apologies and solicitude. He sat on a chair by the porch couch and told Dick how sorry he was. He asked him, "Can I get you a new dog? How would you like a boxer? Or a Dalmatian?"

Dick shook his head.

"I'll tell you what," said Uncle Henry. "Now that I've sold my corn, I'll have a little extra spending money. How would you like a bicycle—a nice big new one, with all the latest trimmings?"

Dick thought for a minute. Then he spoke "No one can love a machine like the flesh and blood of a puppy."

"You don't want a bike then?" asked Uncle Henry.

"No," said Dick. "Nor your tractor either. I don't ever want to drive it again."

CHAPTER X

Market Day

"When do we start?" cried Margy, jumping up and down. "At six-thirty in the morning," said Mom. "We'll have to get up at five to get the chores and the milking done before we go."

"And we'll stay all day?" asked Margy.

"Yes, it will be late when we come home," said Mom.

To sell or not sell the hogs had been a big question. Every day Dad listened to the market prices quoted on the radio. In August the price of hogs had dropped, so Dad decided to hold them until it went up again. Now, in the last week of September, Dad and Uncle Henry decided to sell, and the truckers had come with the trucks.

Outside by the hog-house, Dick and Wilma were helping to load. The March hogs were fat and sleek now and up to market weight. To push them, Dick had been feeding them an extra ration of soaked corn morning, noon and night. Every day Dick had watched them grow fatter.

The truck stood ready by the loading chute, but the hogs were contrary as usual. Buster barked loudly while Wilma and Dick herded them into the hog-house, where they were penned in a small place as near the chute as possible. Then Dad opened the door so they could go right up the chute. But it was no easy task. The hogs did not want to go. They wanted to dash back to the hog lot and clover pasture. Did they love their home and hate to leave it? Dick wondered.

A trucker came up with an electric buzzer and after a touch or two, the hogs began to move. Another trucker came over with a six-foot pole to prod them.

"You don't need to hit them," shouted Dick. "See! They're going up all right."

Dad had a piece of soft harness leather in his hand. He slapped the hogs gently as they passed by. Dick mopped the perspiration from his forehead. Which one was Squeaky? Where was she? He could not find her. She was as big as the others now and they all looked alike. Crowded side by side in the truck, squealing loudly, he could not tell one from the other. Perhaps it was just as well. He did not want to see her anyway.

When both trucks were filled, twenty-five to thirty hogs in each, the drivers drove away. The yard seemed empty and quiet when they were gone. The hogs would have a night journey to the stockyard.

The next morning, the whole family was up at daylight. "Market day"—a trip to the stockyards in Sioux City—was a special occasion, a family occasion. The cows were milked and turned out to pasture, chickens fed and watered and feed for the day put out. The younger hogs left behind were fed and watered. Breakfast over, the family changed clothes. Dad put on a new work shirt and overalls. He was afraid he might ruin his good cloth suit while handling the hogs. Mom and the girls put on their dress-up clothes. They wanted to look well dressed in the city. The boys wore freshly ironed shirts, clean dungarees and jackets.

It was a forty-mile drive and Margy thought they would never get there. Sioux City looked enormous to her when they reached it at last. Margy had never been to the big city before. She began to ask questions. Why were the houses so close together? Why were the stores so tall? Where were all the people going? Mom laughed and had a hard time answering.

Dick kept telling her, "This is a *city*, Margy. This is a *city*."

Dad drove into the city from the east. He had to cross two bridges over the Floyd River, a tributary of the Missouri. Dad spoke of the floods of the previous spring.

"Every trucker has to watch the rainfall," he said. "He doesn't want to be caught on the wrong side of the river with a load of stock. He may be marooned at an oil station for days before he can cross the bridge. That's no fun."

"Where's the stockyard?" asked Dick.

"It's located right between the two rivers," said Dad, "the muddy Mo and the Floyd. They just try to drown out the yards every spring at high-water time. Sometimes the truckers have to drive through water up to the hubcaps on their wheels to get here."

"I suppose the river is always trying to reclaim its old channel bed," said Mom.

"That old Missouri is always flooding," said Raymond. "Remember last spring?"

"Oh, don't talk about those terrible floods," said Wilma.

The Exchange building to the south loomed up large as they drove toward it. Meat packing plants could be seen across the Floyd River. Cattle yards were on the right, and beyond them the sheep barns.

"Is *that* it?" asked Margy, pointing.

"Can't you *smell* it?" asked Dick, teasing.

"Is that where we're going?" Margy went on. "I thought we were going in a store to buy me a new dress."

Mom laughed. "We'll have to sell the hogs first."

"You can call it your *hog dress!*" said Wilma, laughing.

"Are you going to get a new *hog shirt*, Dick?" asked Margy.

"I don't know," said Dick. "Ask Mom."

Dick and Raymond were excited by seeing trucks on all sides, loaded with stock. There were trucks filled with cattle, sheep and hogs going in and empty ones coming out. There were tractors hauling hay in to feed bunks. The air was filled with a combination odor of soap, hay, barnyard manure and chemicals. Dad drove into a special parking place for out-of-town patrons. A man with a cane indicated where he should go. They all got out.

"We made it," said Dad, looking at his watch. "I told Uncle Henry we would be here by eight o'clock."

They went into the Exchange building and waited for a while, but Uncle Henry did not come.

"He must be waiting for us in the hog barn," said Dad. "Let's go out there."

"I'll stay here in the lounge," said Mom, "until you get through and can take us downtown. It's dirty out there—and we have good clothes on."

Mom hung back, but Dad coaxed her. "Come on, Bertha," he said. "Come and see our hogs for the last time."

"Well—as for me," said Wilma, "I won't waste any tears over them."

"We'll take the catwalk," said Dad. "It leads to the hog barn."

"I want to walk on the catwalk," said Margy. "Do they sell *cats* here too?"

Everybody laughed.

They all started up the stairway and followed a covered passage, high enough for trucks to pass underneath. From this elevated boardwalk, with a railing on each side, they could look down on hundreds of pens of cattle. Waves of noise hit their ears—the bawling of cattle, calves and steers, the squealing of hogs, the bleating of sheep and the shouting of men. All was noise and confusion.

"Is this the catwalk?" asked Margy. "Will the cats chase me?"

But no one paid attention to her, there was so much to see. Below them in the cattle yards, men in bright wool jackets and knee boots, riding sleek riding horses, with whips in hand, were driving cattle through alleys into pens. Men's voices calling "Hi-yah!" "Hi-yah!" echoed back and forth. The cattle lowered their heads, dodged this way and that, but finally entered their numbered pens. It was like a rodeo in miniature.

"Say, Dick," said Raymond, "let's you and me stay here and watch the cattle. Say—they sure are bringing in some beauties. Look at that bunch. Those'll be *prime* and top the market sure."

"I want to see our hogs sold," said Dick.

"Aw, stay here with me," begged Raymond. "What do you want to go in that stinking hog barn for?"

"I've *got* to see our hogs sold, I told you," said Dick. "I'll go with Dad."

"I'll stay with you, Raymond," said Wilma. "I'm sick of hogs. And I can keep my clothes clean up here."

Mom, Dick and Margy followed Dad. They entered the second floor of the roofed-over cement hog barn and walked through a long alley. All hogs were received on the ground floor, and kept there over night until assigned to pens upstairs. Dick noticed a large sign and read it aloud:

"USE CANVAS SLAPPERS
Leave canes, whips, clubs in office.
Refrain from kicking hogs.
Use poles only for sorting.
Prevent bruises.   Save Meat.

That sounds like you talking, Dad," said Dick. "Those truckers of ours had buzzers and poles. They ought to get canvas slappers to use."

"Bruised meat brings a lower price," said Dad.

"How do you know where to go, Dad?" asked Dick. "How can you ever find our hogs when there are so many thousands of them?"

Dick stared at the strange hogs in pens on all sides. More and more hogs were being driven in from incoming trucks.

"I'll find ours," said Dad. He located a man from his commission company who told him where to go.

"Here they are," said Dad, "but Uncle Henry is not here."

"Are these ours?" asked Dick.

"Henry promised to be here at eight sharp," said Dad. "We had forty miles to drive and he comes only half as far. Yet we beat him."

"It's no fun to stand around and wait," said Mom.

"Oh, he'll be along soon," said Dad.

Dad started talking to two men who had hogs in the pens across the alley. One man was from South Dakota and the other from Nebraska. But the problems of raising hogs were just the same as in Iowa, so they had a good time comparing notes. Cries of "Hi-yah!" and "Soo-ey!" echoed back and forth through the chilly, drafty building. Close at hand was a "Buyers' Shanty," with telephone booths, where orders for pigs were received from all over the United States.

"There comes Uncle Henry!"

Margy spotted him first and ran up to meet him. He caught her in his arms and tossed her high up in the air. "Upsy-daisy!" he cried. "How's my little Tootie?"

"Good," said Margy, "but hungry!"

"You're late, Henry," said Dad.

"Yes, a little," said Henry. "We had a party last night and I overslept this morning."

"Here comes Red, our commission man," said Dad. "Hi, Red, good morning! Well, we got here."

Red was a short stubby man with red hair and freckles. He smiled broadly and shook hands with everybody, even Mom and

Margy. He motioned to a buyer who now came up. Soon the men were deep in a discussion of Dad's hogs and their merits.

Dick still felt unsure about the hogs. He looked over the fence at them. Both truckloads were crowded together in one pen. They looked different, not the same at all. They were restless and a lot dirtier. A patch of hair had been sheared off their rumps on the right side to identify them. Maybe there was a mistake. Maybe these belonged to someone else. Dick looked at the card tacked up outside the pen. There was Dad's name, the number, description and necessary information. A blank space was left for adding the name of the buyer.

Dick climbed on the fence and called softly, *"Soo-ey! Soo-ey! Soo-ey!"* This was the call he used at home in the hog lot when he fed them. All their heads turned and looked up at him. They squealed a greeting. Dick grinned. They were Dad's hogs all right and they knew him. Then they turned back to their feed again.

"A lot *you* care!" he said in a half-whisper. "All you think about is eat, eat, eat! Well—eat then! This is your last meal."

Mom was right. Nobody could get sentimental over a hog. A calf now was different. A calf was pretty and appealing with its soft eyes and gentle ways. That was why Dick did not want to stay at the cattle pens. Even if they were other people's calves, he could not bear to see them go.

A workman came up with a hose. He turned water on and began washing out an empty pen across the alley. He sloshed running water all around everywhere. It was a big job to keep the pens and alleys clean. Although they were cleaned daily, there was always plenty of dirt from hogs going through.

The first buyer walked away and others came up to Red and gave him bids. Finally, at the highest bid, the hogs were sold. Mom spoke to Dad and said she was taking Margy back to the Exchange building.

"Now, Dick, you come and help," said Dad.

Dick ran over. They drove the hogs out of the pen and down the long alley to the scale house. There they left them to be weighed.

Dick could not help but feel a pang of regret. That was the last he would ever see of them—the last of old Squeaky. It was the last time, too, he would ever make a pet of a runt. He tried to tell himself that Squeaky had been no pet, that she was no different from the others and that he would never miss her. But at the same time it was an awful thought that Squeaky would be on the slaugher block in an hour's time, and no telling how soon after that in a refrigerated car all done up in Cellophane packages or in gauzed quarters. He tried to forget all that. It was better to think of the new litters of hogs that had been coming since August—only to be sold next spring, in April.

"Aw—shoot!" said Dick to himself. "What do I care, anyway! People have been eating hogs since the year one. They'll keep right on doing it, too."

"We'll go to the Exchange building and get our papers," said Dad. "We'll find out what they weigh."

"Did you feed them heavily the last two weeks like I told you?" asked Uncle Henry.

Dick followed slowly behind the men as they returned to the main building. There would be a long time to wait to get the hogs' papers and the check for the hogs. Dick looked at the hogs in the other pens. There were so many they almost made him dizzy.

Suddenly he heard a shriek behind him. It was louder than the squealing of the hogs. It sounded familiar. He turned around to look. Whom should he see but Margy! She was running fast on a cross alleyway, terrified and crying at the top of her voice.

"Margy!" called Dick. "Come here! This way!"

Margy heard him, stopped and looked, then came over sobbing. Her dress was wet and covered with mud.

"Where's Mom?" asked Dick.

"Back over there somewhere," cried Margy, pointing vaguely. "I don't know where. *I lost her!*"

"You lost Mom?" said Dick. "Why, that's impossible."

"We both got lost," explained Margy. "We couldn't find the way out to the Exchange building and we went back to find

you and Dad and Uncle Henry, but the hogs were gone and you weren't there any more. Mom told me to look down one alley and I did and when I went back *she* was gone! I can't find her."

Dick took his little sister by the hand. "I'll find Mom," he said. "You just can't see over the fences, that's all. Stop crying now."

Margy began crying louder than ever.

Dick scolded her. "If you don't quit that noise, I won't even look for her. You sound worse than a stuck pig!"

Margy quieted down to sniffles. Dick walked back a few yards with her. They came on two cats in the alley, licking themselves. Margy stopped to pet them.

"Oh, here are the cats," said Margy. "I'd like one of these."

Dick laughed. "Don't be silly, punkin," he said. "Probably there are rats here and these cats have come to eat them. We've got cats enough at home. You know that."

They looked up and saw Mom hurrying toward them.

"Heavenly days!" cried Mom. "What a place! I'll never come in here again—not if I'm in my right mind."

"Did you really get lost?" asked Dick.

"Well, I got all turned-around," said Mom. "I couldn't seem to find my way out. Each time I turned I went in the wrong direction."

"You were, too, lost!" said Margy. "You said, 'Now I know how Margy felt when she was lost in the cornfield.' "

"Only this place is worse with so many hogs," said Mom. "All these horrible hogs—black ones and brown ones and white ones and spotted ones! All their snouts poking out between the fence rails and squealing and snorting at me. It was like a bad dream.

[155]

I had the awfullest feeling of being lost among all these pens of hogs. I wondered if I'd ever get out. . . ."

"Why didn't you ask some one?" said Dick, smiling.

Mom began to laugh now. "I did ask a man who was shoveling dirt," she went on, "but he didn't know his way out either. He mumbled something I couldn't understand. He just went on shoveling dirt. He looked so black and grimy, I thought, maybe he never *does* get out. Maybe he just *lives* here!"

Dick roared and so did Mom.

"And just look what he did to my coat and dress," said Margy. "He took his hose and splashed water and mud on me. He never even looked to see what he was doing."

"You'll have to go out in the sun and get dried off," said Dick.

"How *do* we get out of here?" asked Mom.

"Come with me," said Dick. "I'll show you. If you just keep going in one direction long enough, you're bound to come out *some*where."

They started walking and soon they could see daylight outside. Mom felt better when she saw she was going in the right direction. They came out on the catwalk again and followed it to the stairs. They went down and came into the Exchange building. Margy's tears were dried now. She forgot about her soiled clothes and they sat down in the lounge.

"Dad and Uncle Henry will find us here," said Mom. "It will be easier for them to find us if we sit down and stay in one place."

"Look at that man's boots," said Margy, giggling. "He's wearing high heels just like a lady."

"He's a real cowboy from Nebraska, I bet," said Dick. "He's got those tight cowboy jeans on and a fancy vest. And look at

[156]

his ten-gallon hat. He looks just like a movie star."

A woman on one side began to talk to Mom. She said she was from Minnesota. Another woman from South Dakota said her farm was part of an Indian reservation. She pointed out groups of Indian women and children in the lounge. "They all raise cattle," she said. "They truck them in here to sell them."

The Exchange building was like a town in itself. Besides offices for the commission firms on various floors, it had a restaurant, barber shop, shoeshine shop, a studio for broadcasting market news and an elevator to the top floor.

All the people who waited were friendly. A woman on the other side of Mom began to talk to her. She said she was from Nebraska and her husband had sent in a load of sheep. She had a girl of ten beside her.

"We flew in ourselves," she added.

"Flew?" asked Mom. "Do you mean you drove fast?"

"Oh no," the woman replied. "We flew in our airplane. We own our own plane. My husband was in the war—he's a good pilot. It takes us only half an hour to get here. If we drove in our car, it would take all day."

Margy stared wide-eyed at the flying girl from Nebraska. Then she whispered to her mother, "She wears blue jeans. She looks just like a plain Iowa girl to me."

"Why shouldn't she?" Mom laughed.

"We saw one load of cows, a mixed bunch, with some sort of skin disease," said the woman from Minnesota. "We wouldn't have cows like that on our place. They won't bring much."

After Wilma and Raymond came back, they all watched the well-fed stockmen come waddling in. They tried to guess how rich they were and whether their wealth was in cattle, hogs or sheep. The men carried papers and notebooks. They slapped other men on the back, calling out, "Hi, pardner!" They talked in loud voices and laughed heartily. Their faces were ruddy from outdoor work.

Raymond was full of enthusiasm over the fine cattle he had seen.

"Boy, they are smooth and sleek, fed to a finish," he said. "Every one in a pen evenly matched, all the same breed and same weight. You never saw such beauties. They'll bring top-notch prices. The commission men can take one look at them and estimate to a fraction just what they'll dress down to. I wish Uncle Henry would go in for more cattle and give up this hog business."

"Give up the hogs?" said Dick. "Oh no, I hope not."

"They've got horses out in the yard there so well trained, they can open gates," Raymond went on. "I'd as soon go out west and live on a ranch. Then I would ride a cow horse and be in the saddle all day."

Wilma laughed. "Raymond still wants to be a cowboy and rope cattle."

"Just like they do in the movies," said Dick. "O. K. Let him go. I'll stay on Dad's farm and help him with the work."

"Those rich cattle buyers have a shoeshine parlor downstairs in the basement," said Raymond, "with fifteen men who do nothing but polish boots! They pay a lot just to get a good polishing job."

"I want a ride on the elevator," the flying girl from Nebraska was saying.

Margy heard her. "Do they have corncribs here?" she asked

her mother. "That Nebraska girl doesn't know much. She thinks she can ride on an elevator."

"She's talking about a city elevator," explained Mom, "not the country kind that takes the corn up to the top of the corncrib. The kind they have here takes people up to the top of this building. You don't have to walk up the stairsteps. You can ride."

"If it's an elevator to ride on," said Margy, "I want to ride on it. If she does it, I want to do it, too."

"Are you sure you won't get scared?" asked Mom.

"I won't," said Margy.

"An elevator ride really means something to a farm kid," said the Minnesota woman, "even to that one who is used to flying in airplanes."

Mom said, "All right then, let's go."

Margy was surprised to see that the elevator was a small room that moved up from the basement and stopped at doors on different floors. She loved to ride. Dick and Wilma went along. On the top floor they looked out and saw the Missouri River beyond the railroad tracks with all the freight cars. Mom pointed out the whole area that had been so badly flooded in the spring. They all rode up and down twice just for the ride. Margy coaxed for more rides when it was time to get off.

It was noon now, and the run of stock for the day had been sold off. The Exchange building became very crowded. Dad and Uncle Henry appeared and located Mom and the children. Dad proudly waved his check and started for the bank to cash it. The family agreed to meet in the cafeteria downstairs for lunch.

In the lunchroom, they had to help themselves to food, fill

their own trays and carry them to a table. Margy had a hard time deciding what to eat. She wanted a sample of everything—but her tray was not large enough.

"Do they make you wash your own dishes, too?" she asked.

Uncle Henry roared with laughter.

The food was good and the meat portions were generous and well prepared. Raymond studied the border of cattle brands decorating the walls. Dick did not talk and hardly ate.

"What's griping *him*?" Raymond leaned over and asked Wilma.

"Gee, does he feel sad!" said Wilma.

"Why?" asked Raymond.

"He's mourning for old Squeaky," said Wilma.

"That mean old hog?" Raymond laughed.

Dick heard them. He looked at their plates. "How can you eat meat?" he asked.

"Why, it's delicious," said Wilma. "My pork chop's so nice and tender."

Dick shook his head in disgust. "She eats *pork* on a day like this!"

Uncle Henry was pleased with the hog sale. "They averaged two hundred and twenty-five pounds. Not bad! Not bad!" he bragged.

"How about it, Mark?" asked Mom. "Did you get a good price?"

"We came within fifteen cents of getting top price," said Dad, smiling.

Uncle Henry teased Mom about getting lost in the hog barn. Mom was good-natured and laughed about it. Each time she repeated her adventures, they grew worse and worse. Then she talked about going to the stores.

After lunch Uncle Henry left and Dad drove uptown. He and the boys took in a western show at the movie house while Mom and the girls went shopping. After the show was over, the girls were still in the stores. Dad was impatient to start for home. At last they came and got in the car.

Dad drove into the truck route along the Missouri River to get out of town quickly. A procession of empty cars and trucks was leaving the stockyards. But Dad could not drive fast. There seemed to be some sort of obstruction ahead and he stopped. A large black and white bull had somehow escaped from a truck. Tail up in the air, the huge animal made a dash for freedom.

There the bull stood in the middle of the street, blocking traffic both ways. People on the sidewalks scurried indoors for safety. An impatient bus driver in a city bus loaded with people, blew his horn. But the bull refused to budge, except to lower his head threateningly when any one came near.

"Gosh! This is exciting!" cried Dick. "What will we do?"

"We'll sit right here," said Dad.

"Now if I just had my lariat," said Raymond, "I'd lasso that bull and show him who's master." The others laughed.

"If that bull charged into the crowd or into that bus," said Dad, "it wouldn't be very funny."

The news had spread quickly back to the stockyard. Two men came dashing up on horseback.

"Now, watch him!" said Raymond. "Even a vicious bull has real respect for a man on a horse."

The men had lariats and soon the stubborn bull was roped, tied to a truck and on its way back to the yards. The bus driver sounded his horn, cars began to move and street activities were resumed as before.

Soon the city was left behind and the Hoffmans were on their way home again. Wilma had spent her money and now her school wardrobe was complete. She talked about her new coat all the way home.

"She thinks it's extra special," said Raymond, "because it came from the city instead of a small store in a small town. There's no difference that I can see. They all come from the same coat factory."

"Except in price," laughed Dad. "She just paid a little more."

Margy did not talk about her new dress at all. Tired out, she leaned against her mother in the back seat and slept. Once she woke up and said, "I didn't feel good all day."

"That's because you ate too much," said Dick.

"No," said Margy. "The smell of the city made me sick."

Mom and Dad laughed.

"Home is the best place," said Dick. "I can't wait to get back to little—" He was about to say *Popcorn*, but stopped just in time. Little Popcorn would not be sitting there on the back steps to welcome him any more. "I want to get back to see Buster again," he added.

As Dad drove in the lane, Margy sat up and said, "I feel good again, now that I'm home."

Chores done, supper over, a tired family was ready for bed.

CHAPTER XI

Before Snow Flies

"I t'll be a big crop," said Uncle Henry one Sunday in October. The whole family had walked out to look over the big eighty. The cornstalks and leaves had begun to turn brown. Soon it would be time to get out the corn picker and harvest the crop. Uncle Henry rubbed his hands together and grinned.

"That's mighty fine corn!" he boasted. "It didn't wash down into the creek either. Now, what you got to say about contouring, Mark Hoffman?"

"I admit it did the trick," said Dad. "Charlie Ruden lost half of that west field of his. He ran his rows straight up and down the slope. That heavy June rain washed deep gullies between

[163]

the rows. His corn there won't be worth picking."

"Now *our* corn," Uncle Henry waved his arm, "means money in our pockets!"

"Money in *your* pocket, maybe," said Dad, frowning. "Time I've paid my loan back to the bank for those cattle I bought, paid all my summer bills, bought winter clothes for the family, fuel for the winter, and counted up the costs of putting in next year's crop—hybrid corn seed, fertilizer, repairs and upkeep on machinery—there won't be a penny left in *my* pocket."

Mom chimed in. "We'll manage to get by, and that's all," she said. "It's an endless circle—work hard all the year and make just enough to give you the necessities and a few comforts, plus enough to put in the crop for *next* year."

"But Bertha," said Uncle Henry, "you can't ask for a better crop than that."

Mom turned to go back to the house. "Don't count your chickens before they're hatched, Henry Shumaker," she said. "It's still out in the field. It's not *picked* yet."

"You'll pick this week, won't you, Mark?" asked Uncle Henry.

"I'm waiting for a hard enough frost," said Dad.

"Don't wait too long," said Uncle Henry. "If snow comes and moistens it, you might not be able to pick before spring. I need my money this fall."

"O. K.," said Dad. "We'll get it in by Thanksgiving—before snow flies."

Corn picking began the next week. Dad decided the fields were just moist enough and the corn was just dry enough. In the morning before he left for school, Dick watched his father grease the corn picker. He helped him take out the old piece of

[164]

barbed wire and put in a new piece on one of the rollers that would pick up the corn. He watched Dad and Raymond start out to the field with it. Raymond had to stay out of school to help.

The corn picker was a fascinating machine, bigger and more fearsome than a tractor, and more dangerous too. Like a huge dragon it moved across the field and gathered up the rows of corn. At the rear a stream of ears poured out into a wagon, while the shredded stalks fell out on the ground behind. What must it be like to drive one of them? Dick tried to see himself sitting up in Dad's seat, proudly making the huge thing go. Somehow he could not get the fascination of the machine out of his mind.

But when he begged to stay home from school, Mom would not let him. The days were beginning to be raw and cold now. She feared a return of his rheumatism, and felt he was better off indoors where there was heat. Dad was short of help with only Raymond. Charlie Ruden came to help one day, then refused to come again. He hated the curving rows and refused to follow them. His boy, Russell, took his place.

On Friday, Elmer Ruden came over after school.

"Did you come to help pick corn?" asked Dick.

"No, I leave that work to the men," said Elmer. "Dad sent me to get Russell. Said he needs him at home."

"He's out in the field now," said Dick. "You can tell him when he comes in. Look what I made."

Dick pulled a corncob pipe out of his pocket. The bowl was a corncob cleaned out to the core. A hole had been drilled in the side, and a dried hollow cornstalk inserted.

"A pipe," said Elmer. "Have you ever smoked it?"

"No," said Dick, "but I've been planning to. I'll go get some matches."

He went into the house and got five or six matches out of the kitchen cupboard. Mom was busy ironing, so she did not notice. When Dick came back, Elmer said, "Where will we go?"

"Come with me," said Dick.

The boys crawled over the fence and followed it until they came to the cornfield. They went out there about four rows and sat down. The corn had not been cut yet. The men were working in the west forty.

Dick tried the pipe first. He packed the bowl with dried corn tassel. He lighted it and smoked for a while. He sucked in and blew out. Then he passed the pipe to Elmer. Elmer put dried corn silk in and smoked. The boys grinned at each other. It was very daring to smoke.

"Nobody can see us here," said Elmer.

"This sure is fun," said Dick, but he did not look enthusiastic. He puffed a while, then choked and coughed. Taking the pipe out of his mouth, he said, "It's got a heck of a taste."

Elmer tried the pipe again.

"I think it's fun to smoke," bragged Elmer. But he, too, began to choke and gag. "Here, take it," he said.

"Say, I forgot, I've got to go and water the hogs," said Dick.

They started back to the hog-house. Dick emptied the corncob pipe and put it back in his pocket.

"Nobody will know a thing," said Elmer.

"Nobody saw us," said Dick.

They both seemed to feel a little guilty. They did not speak of wanting to smoke again. Once was enough. They had cured themselves of the habit before it began. Up by the hog-house,

Dad happened to pass by. He had just brought a load of corn in. He gave the boys a searching look. And did he sniff a little?

Dick whispered to Elmer, "The way Dad looked at us makes me think he knows we smoked. How could he have found out?"

"Search me," said Elmer. "Will he tell your mother?"

"I don't think so," said Dick.

When they saw Dad again, Elmer told him that Russell had to go home.

"I'll send him home after the next load," said Mark Hoffman.

"Can I drive after Russell goes, Dad?" asked Dick.

Dick remembered he had said he would never drive Uncle Henry's tractor again. But he had stayed off it for so long, now he began to be eager again. It would be fun to haul in a few loads of corn. He was tired of doing nothing.

But Dad shook his head. After the corn was elevated into the crib, Dad drove off with the empty wagon to the field.

On Saturday Uncle Henry came out. He met Dick in the barnyard. "How's corn picking doing?" he asked.

"Fine," said Dick. "Just look." He led Uncle Henry to the corncrib. The golden ears were piled high to the very top. "The west forty has nearly filled it."

Uncle Henry rubbed his hands with satisfaction. "Good! Wonderful! That sure is fine looking corn."

"We've got so much corn we don't know where to put it," said Dick.

"We'll have to make some ring cribs," said Uncle Henry. "Maybe three or four. Ring cribs made out of snow fence always indicate a good crop."

"That's what Dad said," Dick replied. "They're about done

in the west forty now, but Dad's short of help. He hopes he can get it all in before snow flies."

"He's short of help—what do you mean?" asked Uncle Henry.

"Charlie Ruden came only one day," said Dick. "Then Russell came, but his Dad sent for him and he never came back."

"I thought the farmers out here like to trade work," said Uncle Henry. "Your Dad has helped the Rudens out time and again."

"Mr. Ruden didn't like the curves," said Dick. "He got mad and went home. Said nobody could drive a corn picker going in circles."

"Why don't your Dad get some other neighbor, then?" asked Uncle Henry.

"They're all busy getting their own corn in," said Dick. "Bill Heiter will come and help when he's done at home and helped out at a couple of other places."

"We'll get snow before then," said Uncle Henry.

They both looked up at the sky. Already it had a dark and threatening look, as if rain or snow were on the way. When Uncle Henry heard that only Raymond was helping, he became very angry.

"That's no way to pick corn," he said. "That's too SLOW. That's as slow as when they used horses and picked by hand."

When Dad came in the next time, Uncle Henry asked, "Why don't you drive the picker and let these boys haul the corn in? How about Dick here? Why isn't he helping?"

Dad hesitated. Then he spoke patiently, for he did not want to have another quarrel with Uncle Henry. "His mother wants him to stay in school. She's afraid he'll get rheumatic fever again."

"Oh, he's outgrown all that," said Uncle Henry. "I used to have aches in my legs, too, when I was a kid. They called them 'growing pains' then. Now they call it rheumatic fever. Look how tall he's grown this summer. The hot dry weather has been good for him. He could at least work a little on Saturday. He can drive a tractor from the field to the elevator, can't he?"

"His mother thinks he should stay inside on these chilly days . . ." began Dad.

"Fresh air never hurt anybody—least of all a corn-farm boy," Uncle Henry went on. "Mark, when are you going to make a man out of that kid?"

The remark struck deep.

"O. K.," said Dad. "Let him bring in a few loads."

Dick was happy again. He knew just what to do. He jumped on the little tractor. How good it was to hear and feel its rumble and vibration beneath him. He had been missing a lot, staying off all this time. When he saw Dad coming in with the next load, he started out at high speed. He had to get there before Dad did, so he could unhook the wagon for him. He changed wagons with Dad and brought the wagon filled with corn back to the elevator. Raymond helped him unload. The end of the wagon was hoisted up and the endgate opened. The corn ran into the elevator and was carried up into the top of the crib.

After Dad took over the picker, Raymond drove the other tractor. Dick liked working with Raymond. The boys took turns bringing in loads. Raymond praised him for the way he was handling the tractor. Dick felt good. He felt every bit as old as Raymond. Uncle Henry was right. He was well again. No more fever and aches and pains. No more crutches for him. The hot

summer had fixed him up all right. He loved the farm and was
going to be a farmer sure. Outdoor life was the best of all.
Why—Raymond was treating him like an equal!

Returning to the field with the empty wagon, Dick liked to
go at top speed. Coming back with the full wagon, he could not
go so fast. But Raymond always seemed surprised when he returned so quickly. He must not keep Raymond waiting. When
Uncle Henry was on the place, everything seemed to move faster.
Uncle Henry was trying to beat the snow. Uncle Henry made a
good boss. He made everybody step around more lively. Dick
just had to feel grateful to Uncle Henry. If it had not been for
him, he would not be driving the little tractor. He would not
be bringing corn in to the crib. He pressed the gas pedal harder.
Yes—his leg was longer. He could reach it now without stretching. He *had* grown taller over summer.

Then Dick gave a quick gasp. All of a sudden he felt a sharp
pain in his chest and things turned black before him. Surprised,
he gave the steering wheel a jerk. He was right at the corner,
turning in from the road to the lane. He shook his head to clear
the wooziness away and held on tight. He felt weak but did not
let go of the wheel. Then he heard a crash and a heavy jolt
behind him. Quickly he stopped the engine and looked back.

"Dog-gone-it! I turned too short!" he cried.

He stepped down and looked. The flare wagon had turned
over and spilled the corn. One wheel was in the ditch. Most of
the corn had been dumped.

His first thought was of Uncle Henry. He hoped he was off
in the west forty and would stay there. But here came Uncle
Henry down the road in his car, as big as life. When he reached
Dick and saw the mishap, he became very angry. He did not ask

how it had happened and Dick was afraid to explain. After righting the wagon and seeing that no damage was done, he said to Dick, "You can get busy now and pick up all that corn by hand. That'll teach you not to be so careless."

Uncle Henry parked his car in the lane, then took the little tractor and went out for the next load himself.

Dick felt sick at heart. All the glory had faded. Raymond would never be proud of him for a stunt like this. He began angrily throwing the corn into the wagon. It would take forever to get it done. His chest felt queer. Now and then he had to sit down to rest. He wondered what Dad would say about this. He hated to disappoint Dad. He would have to explain how everything turned black and he could not see that he was turning too short. He did not want Dad to think he could not turn a corner.

But when the tractor came in, Dad never even looked at Dick. Dad's face was white and he was holding his right hand with his left hand. His right hand was all bundled up in his denim jacket and his shirt sleeve was torn to shreds. Dick saw all this at one glance.

Dad was standing on the tractor, leaning over Uncle Henry who was driving. There was no load of corn behind them. They went right past the dumped wagonload of corn and did not stop. They drove to the house-yard gate and Uncle Henry called. Mom and the girls came running out. Dick heard them screaming. He saw Raymond come tearing up from the crib.

Dick knew something was wrong. His stomach turned upside down. He had heard of corn-picking accidents all his life. Every farmer in the neighborhood could tell of some kind of accident from machinery. Dick hated machines. They killed people. They took off men's hands and arms. They maimed them for life. He hated the corn picker most of all. If there was anything that would keep him from being a farmer, it was a huge big monster of a machine like that. And Dad too—Dad who was always so careful!

At last the boy managed to find his feet. He went to the house as quickly as he could. He saw them all standing there—Wilma and Margy too. He heard Dad say to Mom in a quiet voice, "I guess I got caught this time, Bertha, but it's not bad. I was in too big a hurry. The corn picker got clogged up and I didn't take time to stop the engine."

Uncle Henry began loudly explaining, "On one row, the machine clogged up three times. Mark could only pick the corn one way of the field, it was blown down so bad. After all that dry weather and the high wind, it twisted the corn up pretty badly—"

Mom faced Uncle Henry. "You don't need to shout so," she said. "I know *why* it happened. The men weren't working fast enough to suit you, Henry Shumaker."

Uncle Henry turned away. He stopped talking.

Dad's hurt hand was washed and covered with a clean towel now. Dick could see that Dad's shirt sleeve was torn and his arm was scratched to the shoulder. He did not want to know any more.

"Good thing my jacket was unbuttoned," said Dad. "I stepped out of it easy. That's what saved me."

Dick's knees went weak as he saw the blue denim jacket lying in bits on the floor. He sank down on the couch on the porch. "A guy's just got to watch out," he said to himself.

The next minute they were all gone to take Dad to the hospital—Mom and Raymond with Dad in the car. They headed for town, twelve miles away. Dick and Uncle Henry were left behind. The girls, Wilma and Margy, stood by, speechless and frightened.

When Uncle Henry saw Dick, he pointed out the lane and said in an angry voice, "Get out there and pick up that corn! Don't you ever do a thing you are told to do?" Uncle Henry banged out the door, jumped in his car and drove off in haste.

Wilma and Margy followed Dick to the road. Margy was crying now, but Wilma was angry.

"A lot of help *he* is!" cried Wilma. "Just when he's needed most, he goes running back to town. You don't see *him* staying here and running that beastly old corn picker!"

"I'm glad he's gone," said Dick.

[173]

The two girls helped Dick pick up the corn. They did not talk much. It was a comfort just to be together and to have something to do. At last the corn was all back in the wagon again.

"Whew!" said Dick. "I'm glad that's done." Then he told Wilma how he had turned the wagon over.

"It must have been your heart acting up," said Wilma. "The doctor said—"

"Oh, you're as bad as Mom," said Dick. "Don't tell me what the doctor said."

Wilma spoke gently now. "You go back in the house and lie down. Margy and I will do the chores."

"I'll do chicken chores," said Margy, "and Wilma can do the hog chores."

"No," said Wilma to Margy, "we'll do them all together."

"Oh, I'll help," said Dick. "I feel O. K. now."

"No—go lie down," insisted Wilma.

Dick went in. He sat down on the porch couch. He leaned back on the pillows. The house was quiet. It seemed strange and empty as it always did when Mom was not there. The kitchen clock ticked as loudly as Dick's own heart. How would Dad farm if he lost his hand? How could he get along if Dick was not able to help him? Raymond could not do everything. It was hard to get a hired man. Dad's trouble was so much greater, Dick almost forgot his own. Would he have to tell Dad that his heart had acted up?

Resting on the couch, Dick re-lived the mishap in his mind. How had it happened? It was not his own carelessness as Uncle Henry thought. His heart had skipped a beat—several beats? That was it. That pain, that blacking-out—it was not safe for a

[174]

boy with a weak heart to drive a tractor. He would have to tell
Mom and let her tell the others, even Uncle Henry. Yes, Uncle
Henry would have to be told. And that meant only one thing—
he, Dick, would never be allowed to drive a tractor again.

At last Dick knew the truth. He might as well face it. He was
ashamed of his own failure, ashamed of dumping a wagonload
of corn because he turned the corner too sharp. The work was
too heavy for him. Mom was right—she knew. She always knew
things without being told. Dick would never be a farmer. Why
did he keep on fooling himself like this? Why did he keep on
pretending he was well and strong when he was not? Why not
admit his handicap and accept it? Why not try to live with his
illness until he grew better?

Dick knew what the doctor had said before and would say
again—go to bed, get plenty of rest, no heavy work or lifting.
Be an invalid again. Get up on crutches now and then. Stay in
the house—you boy, who loves the outdoors more than anything
in the world. It was like a prison sentence. Was he to be locked
up for the rest of his life?

Dick began to cry. He knew it was "sissy" to cry, but he did
not care about that now. He was beyond caring about the trivial
meaning of a spiteful word. He could not hold back the tears,
and there was no one to see. After the crying spell was over, he
felt better. He thought of little Popcorn and how much he missed
him. If only Popcorn were here to lie on the bed beside him. . . .
Then he heard a rustle. A wet cold nose touched his hand. It
was old Buster nuzzling him. He patted the dog.

He thought, "I still have my pets. They come and go, but old
Buster is always here. Good old stupid, neglected Buster." He

put his arms around the dog's neck and hugged him. He leaned back on the pillows again. Buster jumped on the couch and curled up at his feet.

Dick thought of Doc Musfelt and his gentle way with animals. But a veterinarian's life is a hard life, Dick told himself sternly. He has to be on call day and night. It takes a strong husky man for that. Cows and hogs were getting all kinds of strange new diseases, so the veterinarian was the busiest man around. No—Dick could not do that.

Suddenly a new idea struck him. He thought of all the pets he had had during the summer and in previous years. "I know what I'll do—I won't be a farmer after all. I'll have a hospital for small animals when I get big—a pet hospital. People will bring me their pets and I'll take care of them and make them well. I'll teach people how to care for them and treat them right. Yes—I can do that. I'd rather work with animals than with machines. Animals are alive."

Then a ray of hope came too. "Maybe if I follow the doctor's orders for a year or two, my heart will get better, I'll outgrow all this and be strong after all." It was worth trying.

Peace came to him with the happy thought. He began to feel rested at last. He dozed off to sleep.

Suddenly he awoke to a loud commotion. He raised himself on one elbow and looked out across the barnyard. It was getting dark. The sun was going down across the valley. Someone had turned the barnyard light on. Men were talking and shouting to each other.

What was that strange procession? Cars and trucks and one,

two, three—four corn pickers were coming into the big eighty. The neighbors had come to harvest the corn. Uncle Henry must have gone after them. Uncle Henry must have spread the news of Dad's accident around to all the other farms. Dick saw Uncle Henry's car come in. He saw Uncle Henry jump out and rush to the field. In no time at all wagons and trucks loaded with corn began to roll into the barnyard. A snow fence had been set in a big wide circle, and corn was being dumped inside. Soon a second, then a third ring was put in place, as the corn rose higher and higher.

Dick had never seen anything so exciting happen so fast. He felt a pang that he could not be a part of it, that he could not be out there helping. He propped up his pillows to watch. It was there that Mom found him, lying in the dark. Wilma must have told her. One look at her face and he knew he did not need to say a word. Mom knew.

Dick put his arms around her and cried out, *"Oh Mom, what would we do without our neighbors?"*

Then Mom sat down and told him the good news about Dad. He would have to stay in the hospital for a while for surgery, but the doctor was going to save his hand. His thumb and fingers were not lost after all. The worst thing was a deep cut from thumb to wrist, but it would heal in time. Wasn't that wonderful?

The neighbor women came bustling in. Mrs. Hass and Mrs. Heiter brought food in covered dishes and started fixing supper and making coffee for the men. Other women came with more food. The kitchen noises and the women's chatter were comforting sounds to hear.

Outside, searchlights were beaming all over the big eighty. The work was getting done and at night too! When the first ring crib was filled, two more were set up. Were they going to fill them all? At last the work stopped and the men came in for lunch and coffee. It was after midnight and they promised to come back on Monday to finish the job. Then the cars and trucks and corn pickers drove off and everything was quiet again.

After Raymond came in, Mom was starting to send the children to bed, when a knock came at the back door. There stood Ted Sanders, holding a dark object on his hand.

"Where's that boy that tames pets?" he asked.

"Here I am." Dick jumped up.

At first he thought Ted was holding a raccoon. Ted had promised to get him one at corn-shelling time. Then he saw it was a large bird. Dick forgot about the raccoon in his surprise.

"It's a sparrow hawk and it's hurt, I think," said Ted. "I was on my way home and I saw something sitting on a fence post.

I was going to let it go, then I thought about you and brought it back. I saw your lights were still on—and I thought you might like to keep it."

"I sure would," said Dick. "I was just needing a new pet. Thank you, Ted."

In the days that followed, Dick was happy to have the hawk to think about and fuss over. He fixed up the white pigeon's cage for it. He set mousetraps in the granary and caught mice to feed it. Every day he left the door of the cage open. The bird was fully feathered and should have been able to fly. It had a wingspread of nearly three feet. But it acted droopy and never tried to fly. Dick studied about it. Maybe it had internal trouble. Maybe it had a nail or a tack inside its body. Would it be wise to operate?

Dick's joints had swollen and he was back on crutches again. Every day he asked the hawk, "When are you going to fly?" He kept it for two weeks. At last a day came when he found the cage empty and the hawk gone. Dick looked around, but he saw no sign of conflict or trouble. The bird's hurt, whatever it was, had healed. The bird had used his wings and flown away. Dick leaned on his crutches and studied the sky. Where the bird went, the boy would never know.

Everybody was happy to see the ring cribs full of corn. Snow came but it was a light one and soon melted. There was still plenty of corn left in the field, corn that was too good to be wasted. The corn picker never picked clean, and many ears had fallen off due to dry weather. Every day after school, Mom and the children wrapped up in warm clothes and went out. Raymond left the wagon a few rows over. They gathered up the corn in piles. They took baskets, carried it to the wagon and dumped it.

Sometimes Dick went along, sat on the tractor seat and watched. Margy stayed with him, and Buster, too, when he was not off chasing rabbits. Dick and Margy had fun counting all the field mice and rabbits they saw. The field animals were glad for a good crop. They were storing away supplies for the oncoming winter. After the picking up was finished, the cattle were turned in to pick up the rest.

Thanksgiving time came, a day of rejoicing and real thanksgiving because Dad was home again, his arm and hand nearly healed. Mom bought a store duck in town and roasted it. She knew Dick could not bear to part with one of his geese just now. Thanksgiving brought Uncle Henry and Aunt Etta and their children out for the day. There were four big pumpkin pies to put the finishing touch to the meal.

Dad and Uncle Henry were friends again, and were making big plans for next year's crops. They talked about sealing the corn in the ring cribs to hold it for a better price. They talked about contouring and decided it had been worth while. Dad did not mention moving away and Uncle Henry seemed satisfied. Dick felt relieved that the farm lease would be renewed. After all, the farm was home.

In the afternoon Margy and Dick popped corn on the kitchen stove for the city cousins. Wilma cooked syrup and they all ate popcorn balls. Dick ate more than anybody else. Uncle Henry laughed and made jokes and everybody had a happy time.

The End

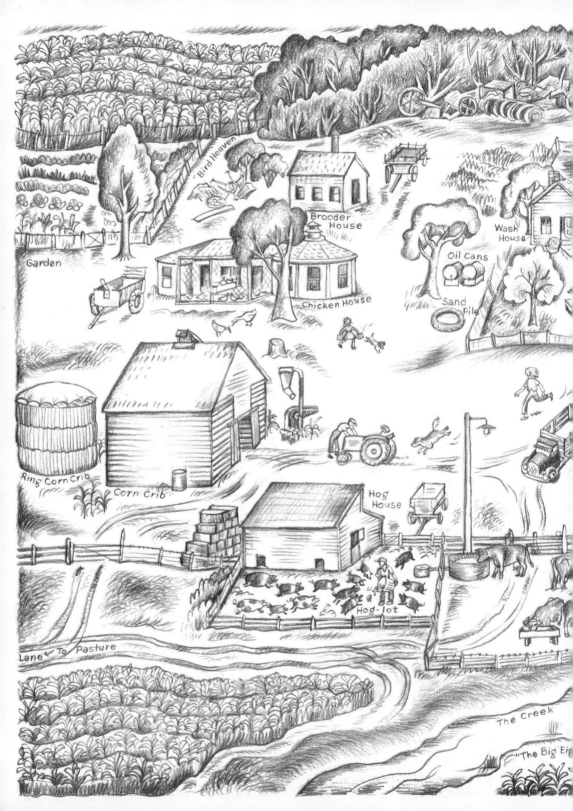

The Grove

House Yard

Barn

Tool
House

Corn
Picker

Cow-lot

LOIS LENSKI